Ouch!

"Oh, come on, Nic. He is my stepfather now, you know."

"Exactly. With the emphasis on *step*. Is he going for a Father of the Year Award or something? Richard never acts like that with me, thank God. And he and Mom have been married for three years."

"Paul's just the huggy type," I explained. "I don't mind it. He's not my father, but he's still a member of the family."

"Wow, he didn't waste any time, did he? He and your mom have been married—what? Three months? And now you're all one big happy family?" Nicole rolled her eyes like she couldn't believe Paul would be so bold.

"It's four months, and yeah, we are one big happy family. You say that like it's a bad thing." I couldn't believe it! Here Nicole and I were, together for the first time in six months, and we were . . . not exactly fighting, but close.

One Summer. One Sleepaway Camp.
Three Thrilling Stories!

How far will Kelly
go to hold on to
her new friends?

What happens when Judith
Ducksworth decides to
become JD at camp?

Can Darcy and
Nicole's friendship
survive the summer?

Summer Camp Secrets

FRIENDS FORNEVER

by Katy Grant

ALADDIN PAPERBACKS

New York   London   Toronto   Sydney

For my own BFF, Susan Moore,
whose friendship, counsel, love, and an
incomparable wit have always sustained me.
And will always—forever.

This book is a work of fiction. Any references to historical events, real people, or real locales are used fictitiously. Other names, characters, places, and incidents are the product of the author's imagination, and any resemblance to actual events or locales or persons, living or dead, is entirely coincidental.

ALADDIN PAPERBACKS
An imprint of Simon & Schuster Children's Publishing Division
1230 Avenue of the Americas, New York, NY 10020
Text copyright © 2008 by Katy Grant
All rights reserved, including the right of reproduction
in whole or in part in any form.
ALADDIN PAPERBACKS and colophon are trademarks of Simon & Schuster, Inc.
Designed by Christopher Grassi
The text of this book was set in Perpetua.
Manufactured in the United States of America
First Aladdin Paperbacks edition June 2008
10 9 8 7 6 5 4 3 2 1
Library of Congress Control Number 2007935963
ISBN-13: 978-1-4169-3578-0
ISBN-10: 1-4169-3578-9

Acknowledgments

Special thanks to my editor Liesa Abrams, whose enthusiasm over this subject matter gave me inspiration through every step of the writing process. I still remember a phone conversation between us when I had only presented her with a few rough pages outlining a story about best friends. Liesa was bubbling over with excitement for this idea, and as I began writing, I kept coming back to her words of encouragement whenever I struggled with the plot or blocked over a passage. All I had to do was remind myself, "Liesa loved this idea!" and I was able to work my way around the rough spots as I wrote. For each of the Summer Camp Secrets books, she has been with me every step of the way, but for this one in particular, Liesa made me feel that this book would become a story that would really speak to my readers.

Thanks to Steve Williams, whose knowledge of rappelling and climbing helped me as I wrote the climbing tower passages. Steve patiently explained basic climbing techniques and answered all my greenhorn questions.

Finally, I want to thank my husband, Eric, and my sons, Jackson and Ethan, for continuing to live with me while I wrote this book. Whenever my frustration levels rose, I would snarl, "These books don't write themselves, you know!" They would immediately pitch in and do their share of housework, laundry, and meal preparation. You guys see me at my worst, and you still love and support me. I am eternally grateful for that.

CHAPTER 1

Sunday, June 15

It was the best day of the year! In one hour we'd be arriving at Camp Pine Haven, and I'd finally get to see Nicole again. I sent her another message.

How much longer 4 u?

Idk
i think bout 30 min
how bout u?

Mom sez 1 hr
u r gonna get
2 PH 1st

Probly

cant wait 2 get off this stinkin bus!

Guess wat

i have a huge secret 2 tell u

"Don't your fingers get tired?" asked Mom from the driver's seat.

"Not really," I said. "You're dropping me off first, right?"

Mom looked at me in the rearview mirror. "No, sweetie. We're dropping Blake off first. We'll get to Camp Crockett before we get to Pine Haven."

"No way! That'll take too long," I groaned as my phone chimed. I read Nicole's text—she was begging me to tell my secret, but I texted back that she'd have to wait.

I tried to reason with Mom. "Look, if you go to Pine Haven first, you'll only have to stop for fifteen minutes. Just unload my stuff, say good-bye, and go. Then you guys can spend extra time with Blake if you want."

Blake was totally focused on his PSP game. I could tell he was nervous about going to sleepaway camp for the first time, even though he was trying to act all cool about it.

"You mean we have to come to a complete stop when we drop you off at Pine Haven?" Paul asked from the captain's chair next to Mom. "Our plan was to drive past really slow and let you jump out. We'll heave your bags to you through the window."

"Sounds great to me," I said, typing a reply to Nicole. She was telling me about the obnoxious girl sitting behind her on the bus who was trying to get everyone to sing "One Hundred Bottles of Beer on the Wall."

"Darcy, it makes more sense to stop at Camp Crockett first, because we come to it before Pine Haven. If we take you first, we'll have to double back."

I sighed. "Well, how long is that going to take? I need to tell Nic exactly when we're getting to Pine Haven."

Mom glanced at her watch. "I'll have you there by one thirty."

"One thirty! But that's two hours away! You said we'd be there in an hour. It's not going to take a whole hour to drop off Blake."

Mom gripped the steering wheel tighter and didn't answer me. Blake didn't make a sound from the backseat. Paul kept quiet too and looked out the window.

Bad news
now mom sez well get 2 PH n 2 hrs!

Y so late?

I tried to text Nicole back to explain about taking Blake to Camp Crockett first, but when I hit send, I got a NO SERVICE message.

"Oh, great! Now I don't even have service!" I snapped my phone shut and tossed it on the seat beside me.

"Oh no, a crisis," Blake said, still not looking up from his game. "You and Nicole can't talk to each other for two whole hours. You'll never make it."

"Relax, kiddo." Paul turned around to smile at me over the back of his seat. "Enjoy the beautiful scenery. Listen to these mellow tunes. Talk to your mom and me. Remember, we won't get to see you two for a whole month."

He gave me a wink and I smiled back. Paul draped his arm around Mom's neck, and she loosened her grip on the steering wheel a little. They were still newly-weds, and they acted like it. Always holding hands and smiling. Saying "I love you" about fifty times a day. It was a little too much PDA for me, but I was glad they were both so happy.

I stared out the window at all the green trees. The road twisted back and forth into hairpin turns as the van climbed higher and higher up the mountain road. I could feel my heart starting to pound. Almost there! Two more hours and I would be back at camp. Back with all my friends. Back with Nicole.

Finally! I'd really thought this day would never come.

From the back bench, Blake looked up and swallowed. He had sweat on his upper lip, and his face was pale. "How much longer?"

"Mom, I think he's going to puke." Mom looked in the rearview mirror.

"I'm not gonna puke. I'm just tired of being in this stupid van."

"Get yourself a cold drink, dude," Paul advised. "It'll settle your stomach."

Blake scrambled over his seat and pulled a can of Sprite out of the cooler in the back.

"Can you get me one too?" I asked.

Just then my phone chimed and flashed a message from Nicole. "Hey! I have service again!"

U still
there?

Ya

lost srvice 4 awhile

Me 2

I texted Nicole again about how we had to go to Camp Crockett first to drop off Blake, but then right after I sent it, I lost service *again*.

I hoped she got my message. Otherwise, she'd get to Pine Haven and be out of her mind waiting for me to arrive.

At least it hadn't been a whole year since Nic and I had seen each other. Over the winter break I'd gone to visit her at her mom's for New Year's Eve. I had hoped Nic could come to Mom and Paul's wedding in February, but her mom said we'd just seen each other the month before. Then we tried to plan a visit over our spring breaks, but they fell on different weeks, so that hadn't worked out either.

I don't think even one day went by when we didn't text or IM each other, but I was still dying to see her. And tell her my secret. I was so excited about it, I had almost given in and texted her about it, but I decided to wait. It would be so much more fun to tell her in person.

While I sipped my Sprite, I kept checking every few minutes to see if I'd gotten service back. I held my phone above my head to try to get a signal. But no matter how much I waved my phone around, it couldn't find a cell tower. About twenty minutes later we were driving under the big, arching Camp Crockett sign. Blake sat forward with his arms propped on the back of my bench, looking at everything out the window.

"You are going to have such a great time. Trust me. Every single second you'll be doing something fun." I grabbed his arm and squeezed it.

"Ow! Stop it, Darcy," Blake said in a really whiny voice that made him sound like he was six, not ten.

"Sorry. Hey, look at the lake. Pretty cool, huh?"

It was actually kind of fun to see Camp Crockett in the daylight. I'd been here a few times in past summers when Pine Haven had dances with the Crockett boys, but it was usually almost dark when we came over.

We found a parking spot along the side of the road and climbed out of the van. All around us were Camp Crockett counselors in red T-shirts, and boys, boys, boys everywhere we looked.

Why had I complained about having to come here

first? This wasn't going to be bad at all.

Mom and Paul left to find someone in charge, while Blake and I watched all the activity. I got more than a few looks from guys who probably felt like I was invading their all-male space. We watched old campers give each other hand slaps, high fives, and fist pounds. That sure was different from Pine Haven, where we all hugged each other.

"Don't worry. You'll make friends really fast," I told Blake.

He frowned at me. "I'm not worried."

Mom and Paul called us over to a group of counselors and introduced us to two of them, Brandon and Rob.

"How's it going, Blake?" asked Brandon, the cute, dark-haired one. He gave Blake a firm handshake. Blake threw his shoulders back a little; he loved the whole male-bonding, handshake thing. Brandon and Rob helped us get Blake's stuff out of the rooftop carrier, and then we headed to Newt Cabin 4.

Camp Crockett had animal names for their age groups—Mites, Newts, Bobcats, and Bears. At Pine Haven we had only three age groups, and the names were kind of boring—Juniors, Middlers, and Seniors. And Camp Crockett called their dining hall the mess and their bathrooms the latrine. I'd always thought it was weird that at Pine Haven the name for our communal bathrooms was Solitary.

Brandon talked a lot, telling Mom and Paul all about where he was from and where he went to college. I couldn't wait to see the inside of the cabins.

I felt like a spy, sneaking around on foreign territory. *Camp Crockett cabins—where few girls have gone before.*

In a lot of ways their cabins were just like ours— wooden buildings with screens all around the top half, two big open rooms called Side A and Side B, and bunk beds and metal cots. Also, there was graffiti all over the wooden walls inside, just like at Pine Haven. Only the outside of their cabins looked different from ours. Theirs were painted a pale green; ours were just plain wood.

"Okay, I did it right this year and packed the sheets and blankets on top," said Mom, opening Blake's trunk so she could make up his bunk.

Now that the excitement of being inside a boys' cabin had passed, I was dying to leave. I was sure that Nicole was already at camp by now, waiting for me. "After this, can we go?" I asked, as softly and politely as I could.

Mom frowned at me as she tucked in Blake's sheets.

After Blake's bunk was made, Mom and Paul wanted to inspect every single inch of Camp Crockett under a magnifying glass.

Finally, after two or three millennia, they were ready to leave.

I knew from experience that Blake's number one priority now was not to cry. I didn't hug him, because he hates when I do that anyway. I just touched his arm. "Hey, I'll see you in about a week at the first dance. Write me whenever."

Blake rolled his eyes. "Don't hold your breath." Then Mom hugged him too tight and too long. What was she thinking? That was a good way to send him right into a bawling breakdown.

Paul smacked him on the back. "Remember what we talked about, okay?"

Blake smiled and nodded. "Yeah, thanks. I will."

Hmm, that was interesting. I guess Paul must've had some kind of heart-to-heart with Blake recently. That was pretty cool. He was good about stuff like that.

I tried not to knock anybody over in my rush to get back to the van.

Finally, finally, finally!

Now I was just minutes away from my first day of summer camp! If I didn't die of excitement on the drive over.

CHAPTER 2

I felt like I was going to explode as we drove down the shady, tree-lined roads toward Pine Haven. This summer camp hidden away in the green, wooded mountains of North Carolina just so happened to be one of my favorite places on the planet. All year long I'd been dreaming about this day. I even had a countdown clock on my blog. When I'd set it up, there were 286 days till camp started. One by one, I'd waited for all those days to tick down.

I tried my phone one last time, but it still couldn't get service, so I gave up and handed it over to Mom. It didn't matter anyway; I was sure that Nicole was already at camp waiting for me.

When at last we saw the wooden sign by the

entrance, I actually screamed out loud. "We're here! We're here!"

"Try to show a little enthusiasm, won't you?" Paul chuckled. Last year he'd come along with Mom to drop me off, so he knew the whole routine.

I gripped the seat and stared out the window, soaking in everything I could—the lake, the tennis courts, the archery range, the path through the woods that led to the riflery range. Senior Lodge, the dining hall, Crafts Cabin, even the infirmary next to the camp office was a wonderful sight. It all looked exactly the same!

"Everything looks so beautiful!" If I had to describe Pine Haven in one word, it would be green—green woods, green grass, a lake shimmering green from all the trees surrounding it. Deep, lush green everywhere I looked.

Mom slowed the van to a crawl as we got to the main part of camp. I saw familiar faces everywhere I looked. As soon as Mom stopped the car, I threw open the door and jumped out.

Lunch had just ended, and everyone was coming out of the dining hall.

"Darcy! Darcy!" I heard people screaming my name from all different directions. All at once I was surrounded by Boo Bauer, Abby Harper, Amber Cummings, Jordan Abernathy, and Molly Chapman.

"Omigosh, it's so good to see you!"

"What cabin are you in?"

"When did you get here?"

We were all hugging and talking at the same time. Then out of the crowd I saw Nicole trying to push through everyone to get to me. "Hey, back off! She's *my* best friend!" Nicole shouted, and everyone laughed and let her squeeze through.

Nicole and I hugged and bounced up and down. "I thought you'd never get here! We got our request—we're in the same cabin again!" she screamed at me.

"We are? Thank God! Who else is with us? Who are our counselors?"

The whole group of us started up the hill. Nicole and I were in Middler Cabin 3 with Libby Sheppard and Jamie Young as our counselors, but none of the rest of the group was in our cabin. During the past two summers, we'd all been together at one point.

"Has your mom left already?" Nic asked me when we were halfway up the hill.

"Omigosh! I completely forgot about them! I kinda abandoned them the second we got here."

Nicole and I left the group and ran back down the

hill to the road, where Paul was unpacking my stuff from the rooftop carrier. Mom stood beside him, shading her eyes and trying to find me in the crowd.

"Darcy!" Mom exclaimed. "Can you please stay with us? You need to carry some things too, you know. Hi, Nicole. You've grown a couple of inches!"

Nicole grabbed my sleeping bag. I carried my duffel and let Mom and Paul get my trunk.

"Sarah Bergman and Whitney Carrington are both in our cabin, but everyone else is new," Nicole told me as we walked back up the hill.

We couldn't stop talking about who was in which cabin, who hadn't come back this year, and which of our old friends Nicole had already seen. By the time we got to Cabin 3, I felt halfway caught up on everything.

"See, I saved the singles for us," said Nic, pointing to the two cots that were side by side next to a set of bunk beds. She'd already made her bed with the same pink and red polka-dot sheets she had last year.

"Perfect!" I tossed my duffel on the empty cot next to hers. "It'll be easier for us to talk after lights out."

It was a madhouse inside the cabin, the way Opening Day always is, with everyone meeting each other, bringing in luggage, and unpacking their stuff. Libby was busy talking to my parents, and I gave Whitney a big hug. She was on Side B with Jamie and three new campers. Whitney was already giving them all a briefing on some Pine Haven traditions. Then I met Patty Nguyen, the new girl on Side A.

Totally unexpectedly, I had a sudden rush of . . . I guess it was homesickness. Only it wasn't for home; it was for the way things were last year with our old cabin. Sure, there were old friends around, but it was a different mix of people from last year. And there were four new people. I just wished everything could be exactly like it was last year.

"I'm on the swimming staff, and my cocounselor, Jamie, is in charge of the riflery range," Libby was telling Mom and Paul. I could tell my parents liked Libby right away. She was really mature; after all, she's twenty-two, definitely one of the older counselors at Pine Haven. Plus, she's got a smile that wins everyone over as soon as they meet her.

I knew Mom wanted to make my bed for me, but I could do it myself. "You guys really don't need to stick around. I know you have a long drive back," I told them.

"And don't let the door hit us on the way out, huh?" Paul said with a laugh. "Do us a favor, okay? Lie to us and tell us you'll miss us?" He put his arm around my shoulders and gave me a squeeze.

I hugged him back. "You know I will. I'm just so excited to finally be here!"

Mom gave me a big hug and kiss. "Remember—you promised us a minimum of two letters a week."

"I know. I promise. And you guys send me lots of e-mails too. Espccially if you have any big news." I smiled knowingly at her.

Paul gave me one last kiss. "We love you, kiddo. Have a great time."

"I love you guys too. Bye!" I walked out the door with them and waved as they walked down Middler Line. I was a little sad to see them go, but I could hardly wait to have my first long conversation with Nic.

When I went back inside, she was sitting on her cot, giving me the look I knew so well—one eyebrow raised, one corner of her mouth twisted down in a frown.

"What's up?" I plopped down on the end of her cot. With my parents out of the way, Libby now focused on helping Patty make up her bunk.

"Paul. Your new 'dad.'" Nicole made quotation marks in the air with her fingers. "All that hugging and kissing and 'we love you, kiddo'? Darcy, how can you stand it?" She grabbed my arm sympathetically. "Who does he think he is?"

"Oh come on, Nic. He is my stepfather now, you know."

"Exactly. With the emphasis on *step*. Is he going for a Father of the Year Award or something? Richard never acts like that with me, thank God. And he and Mom have been married for three years."

"Paul's just the huggy type," I explained. "I don't mind it. He's not my father, but he's still a member of the family."

"Wow, he didn't waste any time, did he? He and your mom have been married—what? Three months? And now you're all one big happy family?" Nicole rolled her eyes like she couldn't believe Paul would be so bold.

"It's four months, and yeah, we are one big happy family. You say that like it's a bad thing." I couldn't believe it! Here Nicole and I were, together for the first time in six months, and we were . . . not exactly fighting, but close.

Nic shook her head and smiled. She must've been thinking the same thing about where this conversation was going, because now her tone was completely different. "It's so great to finally see you! You're already tan. And your hair—I love it longer."

The tan I couldn't do much about. Blake and I both have Mom's Italian complexion. My hair had been short last summer, but I've been letting it grow. It's dark brown and it curls like crazy, but the longer it gets, the more it straightens out. I've always envied Nic's pencil-straight, caramel-colored hair. She can wear it up, down, in braids, or in a ponytail, which was how she had it today.

"Thanks. Cute earrings," I said, looking at the tiny hearts in her ears. "Hey, those look familiar. Did I give those to you?"

Nicole laughed and touched her earlobes. "Not exactly. You left them at my house when you came for New Year's Eve, remember? I was going to mail them to you, but I never got around to it. Then I planned to bring them to camp, but I was so afraid I'd forget them that I stuck them in. Want 'em back?"

"Don't worry about it right now." We both laughed. Last summer I'd come home with half of Nic's clothes in my trunk, and she had a bunch of mine. We swap back and forth so much we sometimes forget which clothes are whose.

"Are you trying to torture me or something?" Nicole asked. "Ten minutes we've been together and you still haven't told me your big secret."

"Oh! Sorry, I was totally distracted. But first I need to go to Solitary. Come with me."

We took off out the door to the bathrooms in the building between Cabins 3 and 4. I wanted to talk to Nicole in private without everyone else hearing us. I went to one of the faucets and washed my hands.

"Hey, this reminds me of when we shaved our legs for the first time." Last summer Nic and I bought plastic razors and a can of shaving cream at the camp store and then shaved in this room. Instead of sinks, Solitary has long troughs all along the walls, so we had to stand at the trough with one leg hooked over the edge so we could reach the faucets. Afterward we had a massive shaving-cream fight. Mom was not thrilled when she found out I'd shaved. She thought eleven was too young.

"Yeah, great memory." Nicole held up both hands like she was about to choke me. "Will you tell me already?"

I grabbed a paper towel from the dispenser, then tossed it into the trash barrel. "Okay. I've been absolutely dying to tell you. Mom and Paul have been talking about having a baby!"

Nicole gasped. "Oh, no! That's horrible! You've got to stop them."

My mouth fell open. "What? Are you kidding me? I am so excited, I could scream! It's incredible! It's amazing! I'm going to be a big sister!"

Nic crossed her arms and glared at me. "You're already a big sister."

"Blake doesn't count. Well, I guess he counts, but it's not like I remember him as a baby. A baby, Nic! We're going to have a sweet, precious, adorable little baby in our family!"

"Precious? Adorable? Do you have any idea how much babies cry? Sweet? Wait'll you get a whiff of the first dirty diaper." Eyebrow up, corner of the mouth down.

"Oh, don't be so negative! Every time I go to the mall, I go straight to the baby clothes section. I hope it's a girl! What do you think of Vanessa? Or Madeline? But a boy would be fine too. Colton. Don't you think that's a cool name? And then there's the nursery to decorate. . . ."

"Yeah, if it's a girl, you'll probably have to share your room with the squealing little darling."

"Who cares! The only thing is"—I grabbed Nic's arm—"Mom's worried about whether she can get pregnant at her age, and if there'll be any complications. I heard them talking about it." Those worries absolutely terrified me.

"Oh, good point. Maybe it won't even happen."

"Nicole! How can you say that?" I was hoping she'd comfort me.

"Darcy, you need to be realistic. Things might not be all sunshine and roses."

"But they might," I insisted. "Mom didn't have any trouble with Blake or me. And she's really healthy. Anyway, that's my big secret." Why did I need to convince Nicole to be happy for me?

"Well, I hope for your sake everything will turn out okay," said Nicole.

Walking back to the cabin, she bumped me with her hip and I bumped her back. Nic and me together again at Camp Pine Haven for another incredible summer. That definitely made me smile.

CHAPTER 3

On the afternoon of every Opening Day, all the campers had to go down to the lake and take a swim test, whether it was our first year or our fifth. I'd always thought that was strange; I mean, if we proved we could swim last summer, why would we have to do it again?

Nic and I had just gotten back to the cabin after our mandatory first-day swim tests when Sarah Bergman arrived.

"Oh, yippee!" she said, spotting the bottom bunk. "I get to fold myself up under here every night?"

At five foot five, Sarah towered over the rest of us. All the girls in our cabin were twelve, but Sarah could've easily passed for fifteen. Her dark hair was pulled back in a French braid. Her forehead was usually wrinkled up in a really serious expression, like she was concentrating on solving a complicated math problem.

"Hey, it could've been worse. The new girl, Patty, picked the top bunk. At least you're not climbing up there every night," I told her. Nicole and I pulled out dry clothes from our trunks and changed out of our wet swimsuits.

"Where's Miss Whitney Louise Carrington?" Sarah asked in a perky voice that was supposed to be an imitation of Whitney. Even though Sarah mocked Whitney constantly, they were still best friends.

"I think she's giving all the newbies the grand tour," said Nicole.

"My mother was a camper at Pine Haven from 1977 to 1981, and my grandmother was a camper from 1951 to 1960," Sarah said in her chirpy Whitney voice. Nic and I fell over laughing. We were definitely in for a fun summer with Sarah around.

"So four new campers? What are they like?" asked Sarah, hunching over to sit on the bottom bunk.

"Well, let's see—I've already mentioned Patty in the top bunk. Seems nice. Kinda quiet, though. She's Asian, long dark hair. I think she's going to be really easygoing. The other three are on Side B with Whitney—Ashlin, Natasha, and Claudia."

"Natasha was on the bus with me," added Nicole. "She sat behind me with that really obnoxious girl."

"But Natasha seems like a real sweetie," I pointed out. "She's very petite, glasses, African American. You can tell she's a little freaked over meeting all these new people. Now, is Claudia the one with dark hair?" I asked Nic.

"No, that's Ashlin. The first time I saw her, I thought she was somebody's little brother. Girls who are that flat-chested shouldn't wear their hair so short," said Nic.

Okay, that was a little mean. "Like you and I have so much to brag about," I said. "So Claudia must be the one with reddish hair—long, parted in the middle. She seems sort of . . ." I tried to think of a way to describe my first impression of Claudia.

"Bored," Nic put in. "This may be her first summer at Pine Haven, but she told us at lunch that she's been to three other summer camps. She's not exactly a newbie."

"And Whitney already has them all under her spell? Amazing!" Sarah snorted.

"Need any help getting your bed made?" I offered.

Sarah groaned and closed her eyes. "Don't bother. I just want to veg for a while." She stretched out on her unmade bunk.

Since we had some free time before dinner, Nic and

I left Sarah to chill while we went up and down Middler Line, trying to find all our old friends.

"Look, there's Alex! And Jennifer's with her!" I said. Alex was our counselor from last year, and Jennifer was our old cabinmate. We all had a happy little reunion in front of Cabin 1.

"You got braces!" I said, and Jennifer moaned and gritted her teeth.

"Two months ago. I hate them."

"Where's Reb?" asked Nicole. That was Jennifer's BFF.

"Not here yet! Can you believe it? She had a really late flight."

"I'm just so glad I've got a whole new batch of *good* campers this year," Alex teased us. "I hope they don't give me as much grief as I had last year."

That homesick feeling hit me again, like a wave in the ocean when you weren't expecting it. If only I could relive last summer, with everything exactly the same.

"Oh, really?" I asked. "Well, Libby Sheppard and Jamie Young are our counselors, so Nic and I got someone decent. For a change." Teasing Alex made the feeling go away a little.

When I looked up, Mary Claire, Nicole's eight-year-old stepsister, was walking toward us. When she saw Nic and me with our friends, she stopped and acted like she wasn't sure what to do next.

"Mary Claire! Hi! Remember me?" I walked up and gave her a little pat on the arm. I'd met her a couple of times when I went to visit Nic. Mary Claire's dad was married to Nicole's mom. Usually it was just Nicole and her mom and stepdad living together, but Mary Claire stayed with them two weekends a month. "Nicole told me you were coming to Pine Haven this year. How do you like it?"

"Um, good." Mary Claire glanced at Nicole, who was still talking to Alex and Jennifer. She chewed on the neckline of her T-shirt, seeming unsure whether she should go talk to Nicole or stay with me.

"What cabin are you in? Who's your counselor?" I asked.

"Junior Cabin Two." The neck of her T-shirt had a big wet spot where she'd been sucking on it. "My counselor . . . um." She closed her eyes for a second, then opened them and smiled at me bashfully. "I forgot her name already."

"Well, when you see her again, check her name tag, all right?" I advised. For the first week of camp, everyone wore name tags. We all had ours on now—they were little oblong slices of wood with a loop of lanyard string to go around our necks.

I glanced at Nicole, who seemed completely oblivious to the fact that her little sister was waiting to talk to her. Younger, I should say. For an eight-year-old, Mary Claire was a rather large girl. She came up to my nose, and by my guess she outweighed me by at least twenty pounds.

We walked over to the others. "This is Mary Claire. She's"—I started to say "Nicole's sister," but Nic stepped on my foot and pressed down with all her weight— "She's a Junior. This is her first year," I managed to say through the pain.

"Well, we should probably go," Nicole said to Jennifer and Alex. "It was great to see you!"

"Hi, Nicole," Mary Claire said as we walked toward Cabin 3.

"Hi," Nicole muttered back, and then as soon as we were far enough away, she snapped at Mary Claire, "Stop sucking on your shirt."

Instantly Mary Claire opened her mouth and released the edge of her shirt.

"You know your dad hates when you do that. We all hate when you do that. Why are you on Middler Line, anyway? You're supposed to stick with the Juniors."

Mary Claire didn't say anything. "I think she wanted to come see our cabin," I said lightly. "Maybe we'll come by and see yours tomorrow."

Nic threw me a dirty look and then turned her attention back to Mary Claire. "Look, you can come to our cabin for a few minutes, but then you have to go back to your cabin. You can't be coming over here all the time. You go to activities, evening programs, and assemblies with your age group. Got it?"

Mary Claire nodded.

"And remember what I told you. We kind of know each other, but that's it."

When we got to Cabin 3, Nicole blocked the doorway with her body and pushed open the screen door with one hand. "Darcy and I are on Side A." Nic pointed to the right side of the cabin. "I'm in that bed. Now go." Nic shooed her away like a puppy. "Make some friends. In *your* cabin."

"Okay. Bye, Nicole." Mary Claire walked away down Middler Line.

"I think she's a little homesick," I said. I looked around for Sarah, but she wasn't in the cabin. Maybe she'd left to find Whitney.

"She'll get over it. Let's go sit out on the hill till the bell rings for dinner."

The hill was like the center of camp. From there you could see the lake, the tennis courts, and the dining hall down below you. Also, the view of the mountains on the horizon was really beautiful.

We found a good spot to sit in the grass. The sun was just below the ridge of the mountains, and a soft, shadowy light hung over everything. Already the whole camp was much quieter with all the parents and cars gone. People were walking around and hanging out and enjoying the nice, cool evening.

"Nic, maybe we should look out for Mary Claire. Make sure she gets adjusted and everything."

"She needs to make her own friends. She can't hang around us all the time."

"Yeah, I know. What was that about you and Mary Claire kind of knowing each other, but that's it?"

Nicole hugged her knees. "I don't want anyone to know that her dad is married to my mom. That doesn't make us sisters, you know. She is *not* my sister."

"Well, why do you care if people know that or not?" I asked.

"I just don't want people to know, okay? I am so glad we have different last names. And we certainly don't look like we're related. No one will ever make the connection between us unless she goes blabbing it all over the place."

"Okay, fine. It's just that . . . remember how scared we were on our first day of camp? And we were ten; she's only eight. We can at least be nice to her when we see her."

Nicole snorted. "We'll be nice to her when we see her. But don't expect me to go looking for her. And don't you dare introduce her as my stepsister to anyone."

"I won't from now on. I didn't know you were disowning her for the summer."

Nic smiled at me. "Oh, not just for the summer. For always."

That seemed like a pretty extreme reaction—to hide the fact that they were related. Mary Claire was kind of a geeky younger kid, but she wasn't *that* bad. Lots of people have geeky little brothers or sisters. But I would keep my mouth shut. And I'd also keep an eye out for Mary Claire. Somebody should look out for her.

CHAPTER 4

When we walked into Middler Lodge after dinner, I had a sudden rush of memories of all the funny skits, games, and contests we'd done in here during past summers. The lodge was a big open room with high rafters, lots of benches for sitting, and a stone fireplace. But tonight it was too warm for a fire, and all the benches had been pushed along the walls to leave an open space in the middle.

All the counselors were lined up in front of us, and they started off the evening program by having us sing some camp songs: "Pine Haven Forever," "Nothing Is Better Than This," and "The Middler Charge." The new campers all looked around and tried to mumble some of the words. I remembered what that was like—to have a bunch of people around me singing songs I didn't know the words to yet.

"Good evening, ladies!" said our counselor, Libby. "We have a lot of activities planned to help you get to know each other. So here's what we want you all to do." Libby explained that we were going to be grouped into categories based on different things about ourselves.

The first game was called "Where are you from?" and counselors scattered all over the lodge and held up signs from different states. We were supposed to get into the group with other people from our state, which meant Nicole and I had to split up.

Then they grouped us by zodiac signs. The groupings turned out to be a good way to get people to talk to each other. I found out that Ashlin, one of the new girls in our cabin, had a birthday two days after mine. The weirdest category was hair color. Nicole and I got to be together in the brunettes group, but it wasn't like having the same hair color gave the group a lot to talk about. The blondes kept yelling, "We're having more fun!" It was pretty lame.

Then the counselors told us to group ourselves by whether we were the oldest, youngest, or middle child in our family. There was also a group for only children. I automatically walked over to the "Oldest" group, but then I had to stop and think about it. I could've gone to the "Middle" group too. Paul has two sons, Jonathon and Anthony, but sometimes I forget that they're my step-brothers now. They almost feel more like cousins than brothers. They're both in college, and we hardly ever see them. Usually just at holidays. I wondered if eventually I would start thinking of Jonathon and Anthony as brothers.

I looked over and noticed that Nicole was in the "Only" group. I didn't give that a lot of thought until I remembered Mary Claire. If Nicole counted her as a little sister, then she could've moved to the "Oldest" too. At first I was a little annoyed that Nicole didn't remember Mary Claire. Or maybe she did and decided to ignore her existence. But then I reminded myself that I'd done the exact same thing—went to the group that matched my biological order instead of my step order. I couldn't really blame Nicole.

When the games were over, we had some time to just hang out. A group of us wandered out to the porch. It was already dark and it was nice and cool. The air smelled like pine trees, and frogs were croaking down by the lake.

Whitney had adopted Claudia, Natasha, and Ashlin, the new campers in 3B. She absolutely adored being a one-woman welcoming committee. "Oh, I'll help you learn all the songs. I have a songbook back in the cabin. Anyone who wants to can borrow it," she was telling them.

While Whitney chatted away, Sarah very quietly walked over to her. Ever so slowly, she held her hand up, opening and closing it like a yakking mouth beside Whitney's face. The newbies tried not to laugh while Whitney kept talking, totally oblivious.

"Oh, this is interesting—there's this one song called 'Camp Days.' My grandmother and some of her friends actually wrote that song. I always get so emotional whenever we sing it!" Whitney sighed while Sarah's hand made sock puppet expressions at her.

"I've been having some serious déjà vu," said Nicole, finding an empty spot on one of the benches.

"Really? Me too. Tell me about yours," I said, jumping up to sit on the handrail.

"Doesn't this remind you of our first summer, when we played that get-acquainted game?" asked Nicole.

"Oh my gosh. It totally does! We were in the same group. And we had to write down all the answers to those questions . . . hometown, birthday, favorite book, favorite food, favorite actor—there were lots of favorites on that list!"

The counselors had put us into small groups and gave us a sheet of questions to answer. Then, instead of reading off what we'd written down, we had to switch papers, and the other person "introduced" us to the rest of the group. Nicole and I happened to sit next to each other, so I introduced her and she introduced me.

"Yeah, and we figured out that both of us had parents who were divorced. You were a real mess that summer. I wasn't sure you were going to survive," said Nicole.

That summer, Mom and Daddy had only been divorced a few months. Everything in our lives was so strange. My parents fought every single time they laid eyes on each other. I would just lock myself in the bathroom and throw up; then I'd come out and try to act like everything was okay when it wasn't. I hated all the fighting and yelling. I like things to be peaceful and happy, like they are now with Mom and Paul. At the time I hated that my parents were getting a divorce. But if I had to choose between my parents living together and fighting all the time or living apart and being happy, I'd definitely choose them being happy.

"Coming to camp was the best thing that ever happened to me," I said. "It got me out of that crazy environment for a while." I slapped at a mosquito on my arm. I should've put bug spray on before we came to the lodge.

"Yeah, and then we met. On the very first night of camp. And we were instant best friends," Nicole added.

"I know! I was so glad I finally had someone to talk to about my family problems. You were a lifesaver."

Nicole laughed. "You were always asking me a million questions: 'Who do you spend the holidays with?' 'Do you have your stuff at both houses, or do you keep everything at your mom's and just take what you need to your dad's?' 'Have your parents started dating other people?' 'Who comes to the parent-teacher conferences?' Yak, yak, yak!"

I smiled at her. "Well, you were the expert. Your parents had been divorced since you were six." Nicole and I talked about everything that summer—all my worries and stresses and fears. All that private stuff about my parents I hadn't told anyone before. "I know this sounds weird, but what if we'd been in different groups for that get-acquainted game? Then we wouldn't have met each other."

"Impossible. It was destiny that we got in the same group. Anyway, let's say we didn't meet at evening program. We had a whole month together. We would've met at some point for sure," Nicole reasoned.

I laughed.

I'd like to think that Nicole and I were destined to

meet and become BFFs, but sometimes I wondered if it worked that way. Mom had picked out two camps for me to choose from—Pine Haven and Camp Willahalee. The main reason I picked Pine Haven was because of the name. It was easier to pronounce.

What if I'd picked Willahalee instead? Then Darcy Bridges and Nicole Grimsley never would have met each other. Was it destiny? When good things happen, it's nice to think that it's destiny, but when stuff goes wrong, you have to wonder why destiny is giving you such a rotten life.

The counselors called us inside for graham crackers and milk, and then we got into the good-night circle to sing "Taps."

Day is done, gone the sun,
From the lake, from the hills, from the sky.
All is well, safely rest,
God is nigh.

"This has been a great first day," Nicole said, as everyone crowded through the doors of the lodge and started up the stone steps toward the cabins. A lot of the old campers were rushing to get to Solitary first so they wouldn't have to wait for a stall.

"Yeah, it sure has. We're going to have an amazing summer," I said. I hadn't had that homesick feeling all evening. I was pretty sure it was gone for good. As much as I wanted this summer to be exactly like last year, or the year before, I knew it didn't really matter. Even though this new summer could never be exactly like the old ones, I was absolutely positive it would be an awesome one.

CHAPTER 5

Monday, June 16

"Anyone who's interested in taking riding lessons, you do need to sign up for those—and it's a good idea to do it as early as possible. I'm going to the stables this morning. Feel free to join me." Whitney was over on Side B getting her troops in order. Jamie loved the fact that Whitney had put herself in charge. The more Whitney took over, the less Jamie had to do.

"Are you going to sign up for riding lessons?" I asked Sarah.

"No. I'm allergic to those hairy beasts. Do you mind if I hang out with you and Nicole?" She glanced at Patty, who was looking for something in her trunk. "You should come with us," she told her. "Stick with the normal people and you'll be safe." She made a smirky face in Whitney's direction.

"If we're normal people, what does that make Whitney?" I wanted to know.

Sarah thought about it for a second. "Deranged. Oh, Whitney darling! I'll see you after your lesson!" she called over to Side B as we all left the cabin.

"Let's go to riflery. Jamie says she needs the company," Nicole suggested.

"I miss Whitney already." Sarah sighed. "Her little turned-up nose. Her dimpled, rosy cheeks. I wish she was right here with us this very moment."

"You two have the weirdest friendship I've ever seen in my life. You obviously like her, but you make fun of her constantly," I said. They were such completely different people, I wondered what had made them friends in the first place.

Sarah covered her mouth in shock. "I would never, ever make fun of Miss Whitney Louise Carrington, third-generation Pine Haven camper!" Nicole and I could not stop laughing. Poor Patty just walked along with us, not knowing what to think.

When we got to the riflery range, Jamie was thrilled to see so many of her Cabin 3 campers. Nicole and I took spots beside each other on the shooting platform, but Sarah and Patty ended up three spots down from us. Since it was the first day, Jamie had to explain to everyone what to do and tell us the rules.

There were bare mattresses lined up across the shooting platform. Prone was the first position in riflery—we had to lie flat on our stomachs and prop ourselves up on our elbows to shoot.

We all loaded our rifles and took aim at the paper targets tacked to the boards across the range from us. "Okay to fire," said Jamie, and then the pops of the rifles firing exploded all around us.

"Hey, I have a great idea," I told Nicole as I squinted through the sight and squeezed the trigger. "What if we ask our parents if you can come home with me on the last day of camp? You can stay for a week, and then we'll drive you home."

"Nope, I can't. My dad and Elizabeth are picking me up on Closing Day. They get me for a whole month after camp is over."

"Oh, yeah. I forgot you usually visit your dad at the end of the summer." Nicole's whole arrangement of splitting time between parents was different from mine. Blake and I spent every other weekend with our dad, but since Nicole's parents lived in different states, she had long visits with her dad during the summer and over the school breaks.

"It's the highlight of my year," Nicole said sarcastically. "Maybe this summer Elizabeth might even let me use a towel. Most of the time I just drip-dry because the towels on the towel racks aren't supposed to be touched by human hands. Their house looks like a model home. Their trash cans are so spotless, I'm always afraid to throw anything away."

Nicole's description of her stepmother always cracked me up. Since I was laughing so hard I could barely aim, Nicole kept going. "It's not that Elizabeth doesn't want me there. She just doesn't want me to eat, sleep, shower, or go to the bathroom. If I stand in the middle of the living room and don't touch anything, that's okay. Wait, that's not okay either! I'll leave dents in the carpet!"

When everyone had finished shooting, Jamie told us to put our weapons down and turn on the safeties before retrieving our targets.

When I saw my target, I burst out laughing. "I only hit the target three times!" I yelled. "That's your fault. You made me laugh too much."

Nicole's score was much better than mine. At least all of her shots had hit the target. We took down the used targets and tacked up fresh ones. Sarah explained to Patty how to score her target.

"You can laugh all you want about it, but everything I'm telling you is true. I hate going there. I feel like I waste the whole month."

"I know Elizabeth gets on your nerves, but at least you get to see your dad."

"I don't need a whole month to visit him. The first two or three days, he asks me all about school and friends and stuff. After that, we're caught up and I might as well go home. It's a waste! I hate it. I don't consider that my home, and I don't consider them my family. Yeah, he's my father, but so what? We're not close. At all." Nicole turned and walked abruptly back to the platform. From the way her shoulders were tensed, I could tell she was getting upset.

We both stretched out on the mattresses and waited for Jamie to give us the order to fire again. Once the rifles started popping, I felt like it was safe to talk without everyone else hearing us.

"But that could change. Maybe this trip, you could try to get closer to your dad."

Nicole kept her eye trained on the sight and didn't look at me. She kept aiming and firing till she'd shot all of her bullets.

"Think of things the two of you can do together— like maybe go out to breakfast. Or go for walks. You could even get Elizabeth in on it. Tell her you need her help to get reacquainted with your dad, so she won't mind if the two of you do some stuff together." Nicole stared at her target, even though it was fifty feet away and it was impossible to tell where any of the bullets had landed.

"It's just a suggestion," I added. "I'm only trying to help."

"I don't need your help."

I sat up on the mattress and looked at her, but she was totally absorbed in putting the safety on. She wouldn't look in my direction.

"Don't be mad, Nic." Now I felt all tense. It was like we had a giant rubber band between us, and if she got wound up, it would wind me up too.

Nicole made a grunting noise. "I'm not *mad*. What a stupid thing to say."

"Okay to retrieve your targets," said Jamie, and Nicole jumped off the platform and had her target down before I even had a chance to stand up. I ran to catch up with her, but she was so busy staring at her target, she didn't even acknowledge my existence.

"Wow. Good score. You beat me again."

Nicole walked just enough ahead of me so that she wouldn't have to look at me.

"You know how sad it makes me to leave camp in July?" I said. "It's bad enough that we have to say good-bye to each other, but it's even worse when I think about you going to your dad's and being all depressed and lonely. I can't stand that."

Nicole spun around and glared at me. One eyebrow shot up. "I am not depressed and lonely. Stop feeling sorry for me. I *said* it was a waste of time. There's a big difference."

Nicole and I walked down the wooded path together, but I didn't bother to say anything. I was getting tired of having my head bitten off repeatedly. Nicole held her paper targets in front of her and studied them like a road map. When Sarah and Patty caught up with us, they immediately knew something was up.

"I sense . . ." Sarah started before I gave her a look. "I sense an attack of hay fever coming on! Hurry, Patty! Help me find some Kleenex before my sinuses explode!" She rushed Patty up the path ahead of us.

"I'm sorry," I said finally. I didn't know what else to say.

Nicole rolled her eyes in disgust. "If anyone should apologize, it should be me."

"You? Why you?" I asked.

"I'm sorry I don't have a perfect family who takes

walks together and goes out to breakfast and chats about how great our lives are." She swatted tree branches out of her way as she walked along the overgrown path.

It was such a ridiculous comment, all I could do was laugh. "Nic, you have to be kidding me. If you think *my* family is perfect after all that stuff I told you . . . remember, you know all my darkest secrets. You're the only one who knows that stuff."

"Just don't give me any advice on how to deal with my family, all right?"

"Fine." We didn't say anything for several long minutes. I'd always turned to Nic for advice about my family troubles. Why was it so wrong now that I was trying to help her?

"It's all your fault that the plan didn't work out," I blurted out suddenly.

Nicole turned around and stared at me. "What are you talking about?"

"The plan. If you'd followed the plan the way you were supposed to, we'd go home together at the end of camp. As sisters." I tried to look serious.

Nicole's mouth twisted into a smile when she realized what I was talking about. "My fault the plan didn't work? No way! *You* didn't get your mom to wear the right dress!"

"*You* were supposed to make sure your dad stopped in town to eat lunch at that little restaurant my mom liked so much. And you should've warned him not to wear white socks with sandals!" I burst out laughing, remembering the first time I'd met Nicole's dad.

Nicole covered her face with her hands. "Omigod. White socks with sandals. And he was wearing that stupid plaid shirt that looked like a picnic blanket." By now we were both cracking up.

"It was a total and complete failure. My mom was supposed to take one look at your dad when they came to pick us up from camp and fall for him like a rock. We blew it, Nic!"

"*The Plan,*" said Nicole dramatically. "I wonder how many hours we spent that summer working on the plan?"

Sometime during our first summer together a bolt of lightning came out of the sky, and I had an absolutely astounding, brilliant idea. All Nic and I had to do was get our parents together and let them fall in love with each other so that we could become sisters. At that time her dad was still single, and even though Paul was one of Mom's many online "friends," I'd never even met him. It seemed like our parents really needed our help with their love lives. It was pretty ridiculous, but we were ten.

"I still have that notebook," I told Nicole. "With all our lists. Sylvia's likes. Dan's likes. Sylvia's dislikes. Dan's dislikes."

We got to the end of the path, and Nicole collapsed in laughter when we sat down in the field of grass by the edge of the road. "I put down 'tomatoes,' 'country music,' and 'reality TV shows' as my dad's dislikes! And you were so worried because your mom puts tomato sauce in everything!"

I smiled at the memory. "We were absolutely convinced they were a perfect match. Except for the tomato sauce."

"I can't believe your mom ruined everything and married Parrothead instead." Nicole stretched out in the grass and covered her face with her arms to keep the sun out of her eyes.

I was going to say something about her dad screwing things up too by marrying Elizabeth, but I stopped myself.

Parrothead. That was Paul's screen name when he and Mom were IMing each other. That name seemed so creepy to me. But his wasn't the only weird screen name. *Crazeecapricorn. Chicago_son. Sirluvalot.* Gross. Two years ago I thought my whole life depended on keeping Mom from chatting with all those online weirdos.

How could I have known that Paul would turn out to be such a nice, normal guy and that "Parrothead" just meant that he liked Jimmy Buffett's music? And then last summer he and Mom took Blake and me to a Buffett concert, and everyone was wearing grass skirts and funny hats and playing with beach balls; we all decided to be parrotheads after that.

"Why did it work in *The Parent Trap*, but it didn't work for us?" I wailed.

"Because that's Disney. And real life is nothing like Disney," said Nicole.

"Yeah, I know." I sighed, trying to act like I hadn't heard the bitter tone in her last remark. I was just glad that I'd been able to steer the conversation toward a happy memory for a while. I didn't want to bring up her father and Elizabeth again. It seemed like it was better to avoid that subject as much as possible.

What if life *was* like a Disney movie, though? Would it have been so unbelievable for Nicole's dad to marry my mom and for us to become stepsisters? It was just too perfect.

But things were pretty good now. I've always been glad that Mom picked Paul instead of Crazeecapricorn or any of the others. But what if she'd never even wanted to meet Paul? What if she'd met Sirluvalot instead and he ended up being my new stepfather?

"Our families sure are crazy. I'm glad we have each other," I told Nicole. "At least destiny worked for us, even if it totally bombed at bringing our parents together."

Nicole had a big smile on her face when she sat up. "I miss the plan. Maybe we should come up with another project for the summer."

"Like what?"

"Like figuring out how to get my dad to divorce Elizabeth! Just kidding. Let's go to canoeing and we'll think about it."

CHAPTER 6

Thursday, June 19

After lunch there was an enormous traffic jam on the dining hall porch as we all crowded around the rows of wooden cubbies to check our mail. Already I could see a few pieces of mail peeking out of my cubby.

I skimmed the printout of Mom and Paul's e-mail first, thinking there might be some big announcement. There wasn't. In a way, I wished I didn't know about the whole baby-planning thing. That way, if it never happened, I wouldn't be so disappointed.

"How many letters did you get today?" Nicole asked as we squeezed through the crowd and walked up the hill toward the cabin.

"Three. An e-mail from Mom and Paul, one from my dad, and a card from my friend Olivia."

"Lucky you," said Nicole, unfolding the printout of the e-mail she'd found in her box. I always got more mail than Nic did, and she always seemed bothered by that. I couldn't help it—either my family was really big on writing or hers wasn't.

"Hi, Nicole. Hi, Darcy," I heard someone say behind us.

It was Mary Claire. Another Junior girl was with her.

"Hi, Mary Claire. Who's your friend?" I asked.

"Alyssa. She's in my cabin. She's on the top bunk, and I'm on the bottom."

"That's cool. So how do you like camp?" I asked.

"Good," said Mary Claire. The neck of her T-shirt wasn't wet today, but it did look all stretched out and wrinkled. While Nicole read her e-mail, I made small talk as we walked up the hill together.

Alyssa was a lot smaller than Mary Claire. She had long hair that hung in her eyes, and enormous front teeth. It looked like she'd gotten her permanent teeth before her mouth was big enough for them.

"Mary Claire has been talking about being friends with Middlers, but I thought she was lying," said Alyssa.

"No, she really does know both of us," I told Alyssa.

"Huh. I'm surprised Spud has friends."

"Spud?" I asked.

Mary Claire smiled nervously. "That's my nickname. Alyssa gave it to me."

Alyssa laughed. "Yep. This girl loves her taters. You should've seen how many she ate the other night. Hardly left any for the rest of us. Right, Spud?" She poked Mary Claire's belly. Alyssa was undoubtedly the most annoying kid I'd ever met in my life.

We were at the top of the hill now, so I said goodbye to them, and Nicole and I headed toward Middler Line.

"Mary Claire has a new friend," I said, as if Nic had missed the whole conversation completely.

"Thank God." Nicole glanced up from her e-mail. "Mom writes such great letters. It's all about the fight she had with Richard over the credit card bills. He's using the wrong cards again, the ones with the really high interest rates." Nicole offered me the paper. "Want to read it? It's riveting."

"Uh, no thanks." My parents never wrote me about their credit card bills. Mom told me about cute things the dogs did, and Paul had written me a funny poem. Daddy's e-mail was a bit of a surprise. He said he'd bought a motorcycle! Good thing Mom wasn't still married to him. Actually, if they were still married, she probably wouldn't have allowed something like that.

"Don't worry. You're not missing anything," Nic assured me. As we walked into the cabin for rest hour, she crumpled the paper up and dropped it into the trash can by the door. I always thought it was weird that Nicole threw most of her mail away right after she read it, but now I could sort of see why.

I decided to go ahead and write Daddy and Mom and Paul back right away, since last summer I'd gotten lots of complaints from them about not writing often enough. Sarah had her bat mitzvah coming up in November, so she spent rest hour studying her Torah passage.

When rest hour ended, Nic and I met up with a group to go to Angelhair Falls. About six or seven of us showed up for the hike, along with Rachel, one of the hiking counselors. It was a fun tradition to go to the falls during the first week of camp, so I'd really been looking forward to this.

It was an absolutely beautiful hike through the woods. As we walked along, I felt like we were inside a green, leafy cavern. Sunshine came filtering through the branches overhead and made a pattern of dancing light on the leaf-covered ground. I loved being totally surrounded by trees like this. It always made me feel like I was a part of nature.

"I can't believe how beautiful everything is around here," said a newbie, coming up beside Nic and me. "It's nothing like living in the city."

"Just wait till you see the falls," I told her.

"Oooh! I can't wait. I'm Brittany, by the way." She was really bubbly and smiley.

"I'm Darcy, and this is Nicole. So how do you like Pine Haven so far?"

"Oh, I love it! Everyone's so friendly. How many years have you been coming here?"

"This is my third," I said.

"Hey, I have a question for you. Why do they call the bathrooms here Solitary?"

I laughed. "I honestly don't know. I wondered the same thing my first year too."

"Hmm. Interesting. I figured there was some story behind that name. Well, what about the CATs? Where'd they get that name?"

"Oh, I do know the answer to that one. It stands for Counselor Assistant in Training," I explained. The CATs were the oldest group of girls—the sixteen-year-olds who weren't old enough to be counselors yet.

"How much farther to the falls?" asked Erin Harmon, giving Rachel a wink.

"How much farther? How much farther?" Rachel teased. "Are you tired already?"

"No, we're not tired. Just eager to get there," said Brittany.

"I'll let the rest of you tell me when we're getting close to the falls," said Rachel. "Whoever's the first one to hear it will get a prize." She winked back at Erin.

We tried not to crunch through the leaves and underbrush too loudly, so that we'd be able to hear the sound of the falls.

"Pretty annoying, huh?" Nicole whispered to me as we walked along.

"What is?" I asked.

Nic jerked her head in Brittany's direction. Now she was just ahead of us, talking to a couple of other girls.

I shrugged. What was so annoying? "She's just being friendly," I whispered back. Actually, I'd been pretty impressed that one of the newbies was so outgoing. Usually they waited for us to talk to them.

"You call it friendly? I call it pushy," Nic murmured. "I hope she gets the prize."

We hiked for another half hour or so until one of the newbies near the front of the group stopped. "Wait. I think I can hear running water." We all paused and listened. The sound of a little babbling stream came through the trees.

"Kayla gets the prize, since she was the first one to hear it," announced Rachel. Erin dropped back so she could walk next to Nic and me. "Be ready for the signal," she told us. Nic and I nodded.

We cut through the trees until we came to the falls, which were tiny by most waterfall standards. The drop from the top of the rocks where the falls formed to the pool of water below was no more than ten or twelve feet.

"I was expecting something a little bigger," Brittany admitted.

"See why these are called Angelhair?" asked Rachel, pointing to the way the rocks made the water pour over the edge in threadlike streams.

"Okay. What's my prize?" Kayla wondered.

"We throw you in!" shouted Rachel, rushing at her. When she said that, Erin, Nic, and I rushed forward too, and we grabbed her by the arms and legs before she knew what was happening.

We carried her down to the edge and started swinging her back and forth over the water as she screamed her head off.

"One . . . two . . . ," yelled Rachel, and then on

three we laid her down gently in the damp moss by the stream. A newbie always got this joke played on her, because the rest of us knew to keep our mouths shut.

The newbies who were watching all cracked up over the sight. It took them a couple of seconds to figure out the inside joke. Kayla sat up and heaved a sigh. She still had a look of terror on her face. "Now I'm wet," she said, inspecting the moss underneath her.

"This is a great home for Nellie," said Rachel, slipping her backpack off her shoulders and unzipping it. She took out a glass jar with an orange newt inside. "I had to catch this little critter yesterday. Remember? It had a part in last night's skit for evening program." We all watched while she unscrewed the lid and shook it gently. The little salamander crawled out and paused on the carpet of moss before disappearing under a rock.

Everyone was peeling off shoes and socks to wade into the rushing stream. "Hey, Darcy, Nicole—come on in!" called Brittany. She stood in the stream with her arms stretched out, desperately trying to keep her balance on the slippery, moss-covered rocks.

"Sure!" I yelled. I couldn't wait to let the cold water cool off my sweaty feet.

The water was so numbingly cold that it made my legs ache all the way up to my knees. I could feel the pull of the current swirling past my ankles. We waded and splashed around till we were soaking wet. It was so much fun, but I looked around and realized that Nicole was still sitting alone on the bank. I didn't even notice that she hadn't followed me in.

"Aren't you getting in?" I called to her. But she just shook her head and didn't move.

I felt like I should get out and go sit with her, but this was what we came for. Yeah, the water was icy cold and the rocks were so mossy and slippery that it made wading pretty treacherous, but nobody really cared. I stayed in for a few more minutes, then got out and grabbed my shoes.

"It was great! Really refreshing," I said, sitting down on the bank by Nicole. I wiggled my wet feet into my dry, dusty socks.

She didn't say anything.

"What's wrong?"

"Nothing." She watched the water spilling over the rocks and wouldn't look at me.

"You sure?"

Nic nodded. She did that sometimes, got moody and quiet. I knew something was wrong, but I wasn't sure what. Did it annoy her that I'd spoken to Brittany? That seemed like such a trivial thing. Or was it that I'd gone in with everyone else instead of staying with her? Or something else completely, maybe even something that had nothing to do with me?

"I'm freezing! I'm soaked!" Brittany shrieked as she ran up to us and grabbed her shoes. "This is so much fun!"

I smiled and nodded, but I didn't talk to her this time. It made me feel silly, not talking to her in case that was what was making Nic mad. I didn't want to be rude.

Here we were on this beautiful, sunny day, surrounded by woods next to a scenic little waterfall. It was almost perfect.

Except for the dark little storm cloud beside me. I hoped that the weather would be nicer tomorrow.

CHAPTER 7

Saturday, June 21

On Saturday, Nicole and I skipped afternoon activities to make sure we each got a hot shower. Usually on the first Saturday night of every camp session, Pine Haven would have a dance with the boys from Camp Crockett. *Usually*, but not always. The counselors had an infuriating habit of not announcing dances till the last minute. They wanted us to go to activities instead of spending the whole afternoon getting ready.

Nic and I weren't willing to take a chance, and we weren't the only ones who assumed there was a dance with Camp Crockett tonight. Everyone was busy getting ready.

"Have you decided what you're going to wear?" I asked Nicole when we got back from the showers.

"Well, these jeans"—she pulled a pair of denim capris from her trunk—"and I was thinking this shirt." She opened my trunk and searched around until she found my pink-and-white American Eagle rugby. She laid the clothes out on her cot for my approval. "Cute, huh?"

"Oh, so you're assuming *I'm* not wearing that shirt tonight?" I teased her.

"I know you're not wearing it because you're wearing this instead." She took my flouncy khaki skirt out of my trunk and draped it across my bed. Then, from her trunk, she pulled out a violet tunic with a scoop neck and puckered sleeves. She knew that was my favorite shirt of hers. "There. Now we both know what we're wearing, and that's always the hardest part." Nicole had been in a good mood all day. Times like this reminded me of why she was my best friend.

"Are you going to wear my earrings?" I asked, since she still had my little hearts in, the same ones she'd been wearing since the first day.

"If you don't mind."

"Of course not. If you'll let me borrow your shell necklace. I just wish we lived close enough that we could swap clothes and jewelry like this all year long."

Whitney came in dressed in riding pants and boots and gave us a quick hello.

"Where's Sarah?"

"Still in the showers. How was your lesson?" I asked her.

"Fine, thanks. Caroline says my posture during jumps is exceptional." She pulled out her hair elastic and shook her head so her reddish blond hair fell across her shoulders.

Just then Sarah walked in the door dressed in her robe. "What did I miss? What's exceptional?"

"Nothing. Caroline just complimented me on how well I took my jumps today."

Sarah clapped her hands. "Did she also tell you your bowing was exceptional? And your handstands? And every single thing about you?" Whitney had always made sure we knew about her multiple extracurricular activities—violin, gymnastics, not to mention all of her riding accomplishments.

"As a matter of fact, she did," said Whitney, not even looking at Sarah. "I'm glad you're all here. I've been waiting for a chance for the old campers to be alone. We need to talk about the very serious problems occurring right now."

Sarah rubbed her wet hair with a towel. "You're right. But which problems are you referring to? Global warming? Or the lack of blueberry syrup at breakfast?"

I had to laugh, even though I tried hard not to. This morning Whitney had been very upset that only maple syrup was served to pour over the blueberry pancakes.

Whitney pointed at Sarah. "Global warming is everyone's problem, Sarah. We all live on this planet, but that's not what I want to talk about. It's Cabin Three and all our troubles."

"Oh, you mean the whole Jamie thing again?" I asked. Jamie, as a first-year counselor assistant, was turning out to be a major disappointment for Whitney. Jamie didn't stress over cleaning the cabin for inspection every morning or making sure no one was cabin-sitting instead of going to activities. Basically, Jamie didn't stress over anything. Why should she when she had Whitney around to do it for her?

"Well, yes. There's that. She has no respect for order and discipline. She doesn't even care if we talk during rest hour. And she offered us M&M's and Starbursts the other night when we all know candy's not allowed!"

Sarah gasped. "She should be fired! What was she thinking? Doesn't she know we're all in our cavity-prone years?"

Whitney ignored Sarah's remark and kept going. "And then there's Natasha and Ashlin. They've completely shunned Claudia."

"Whitney—that is *so* not true! Natasha and Ashlin are too nice to shun anyone," I assured her.

Whitney let out a long, frustrated sigh. "That's not all. Have you noticed how Claudia marks every day off the calendar? She's been counting down the days till camp is over since the first day! That girl is literally wishing her life away."

Sarah collapsed on her bottom bunk and draped her arm across her face. "You're right! The whole cabin is falling apart!"

"We are the leaders here," said Whitney, standing up to make her point. "The four of us, being old campers, need to take charge and address these problems. Are you with me?"

Sarah waved at her from her bunk. "We sure are. Thank you so much for bringing all this to our attention." She sniffed loudly. "Do I smell horse manure?"

"No, you don't. I always scrape my boots before I leave the stables. So, here's my plan. The four of us will—"

"Whitney, darling, did you see the line for the showers? If you get down there now, you'll only have an hour wait. Tell us your plan when you come back."

Nicole nodded. "Good idea. Darcy and I love plans. We're very good at them."

Whitney let out a little sigh. "Fine. It's just that the four of us need to be a united front. I hope we all agree about that."

"Absolutely," I assured her.

Whitney went over to Side B to get her towel, soap, and shampoo.

Once she was out the door, Sarah sat up on her bed and looked at us. "Is anyone else relieved she's gone?" she asked.

"Yes!" I shouted.

"Me too! Sarah, doesn't she drive you insane?" asked Nicole.

"You guys know I love her to death, but lately . . ." Sarah trailed off.

"She's just disappointed that she hasn't been able to turn the four newbies into Whitney clones," I said, laughing. As far as I could tell, all the new girls were getting along just fine. Natasha and Ashlin had become instant best friends, Claudia was busy with some swim class, and Patty spent all her time at canoeing. They didn't need Whitney directing their lives.

Nicole stood up and threw her shoulders back. "My posture is exceptional. And I placed second on vault and fourth on bars at regional this year."

Sarah ran her comb through her wet hair. "She's

always been a control freak. And she brags too much. None of this is new. But lately, she's really starting to get on my nerves. Do you see what I have to deal with?"

"Dump her," Nicole said. "I couldn't stand to spend two minutes with her."

"Yeah, hang with us instead." I picked up my pillow and hugged it. There was something so deliciously fun about gossiping. I felt so connected to Sarah and Nic at this moment. "Why are you even friends with her, Sarah? I've never been able to figure that out. You two are so different."

Sarah's forehead wrinkled while she thought about that. "I don't know. Because last summer our beds were right next to each other. And making fun of her is what gives my life meaning. But . . ." She shook her head. "Things are different this summer. I used to think she was funny. Now I just think she's annoying."

I supposed that made sense, that they got to be friends because Whitney was close by—literally. It was like me being friends with Emma Barrett in fifth grade because her desk was in front of mine. But last year we were in different classes, and we barely spoke to each other. It wasn't the same type of friendship that Nic and I had, where we both had so much in common.

"Seriously—Nic and I are here for you. I'm sure the

Crockett boys will be falling all over Whitney, so while she's busy being prom queen, you can chill with us tonight," I said.

"She is my best friend, but there are times when I want to . . ." Sarah picked up her pillow and crept toward Nicole, then sprung on her, trying to press the pillow over her face. Nic screamed, and I bopped Sarah with my pillow. We were all cracking up when Natasha and Ashlin walked in.

"Oh, hi! We're just gossiping," said Sarah. They smiled at us before going over to Side B as fast as they could. All the newbies seemed to think we were weird, for some strange reason.

Soon everyone showed up, and the cabin was a madhouse while we all got ready. I was looking forward to seeing Blake tonight. I'd written him two letters this week, and he'd sent me one postcard.

Darcy,

   My counsillor is making us write letters to our family. C U at the dance. Bye.

He hadn't even signed his name. I couldn't wait to hear how his first week of camp had gone so I could give Mom, Paul, and Daddy a full report.

Whitney came back from the showers and went straight to Side B to get dressed. Even though we'd made fun of her, I was still curious about what she wanted us to do to solve Cabin 3's "problems," so when the bell rang for dinner, we all walked to the dining hall together.

"Whitney, how about telling us your plan now?" said Nicole, her voice dripping with sarcasm.

Whitney looked at us. "I think the four of us should set an example. We should make a point of never talking about other people behind their backs." She looked directly at me in a way that made my blood turn to ice water. "I know I brought up the problems we're having, but I only want to make our cabin the best it can be. Maybe I don't always put things the right way, but I always try to be nice to everyone."

Sarah looked at me with this totally horrified expression.

Whitney kept going. "The other part of the plan is that we shouldn't make fun of people just because they happen to be talented. *I* would never laugh at Natasha if she told me she'd scored a bull's-eye in riflery. And I wouldn't say mean things about Patty if she mentioned that she was going on a river trip with the canoers." Whitney's voice cracked when she made that last comment, and I looked away. If she was going to break down, I didn't want to see it.

Sarah, Nic, and I didn't say a word. I could not believe what was happening. I felt like a cockroach. Why didn't Whitney just step on me and put me out of my misery?

"The other part of the plan is that we should be honest with each other. Sarah, if you were doing something that really bothered me, I would find a way to talk to you about it. But I would do everything I could not to hurt your feelings."

I looked up and saw that Whitney's chin was quivering. Sarah opened her mouth to say something but then closed it. She looked like she'd been struck by lightning.

Whitney let out a long, shuddering sigh. "So that's my plan."

There was the longest, most humongous silence I'd ever heard in my life. It pressed on us like it weighed five thousand pounds. It felt like a black, hairy, suffocating nightmare.

Somebody say something! I psychically shouted at Sarah and Nicole. But apparently they couldn't hear me.

We walked into the dining hall and took our seats around Cabin 3's table. Whitney calmly put her napkin in her lap without looking at any of us.

Libby poured bug juice into plastic cups and passed them around the table. "Why is everyone so quiet?"

Everyone else started talking, but Sarah, Nicole, and I kept our mouths shut. Too bad we'd learned that lesson a little too late.

CHAPTER 8

When we walked into Camp Crockett's dining hall, I looked around for Blake. I saw him in the crowd of boys and motioned for him to come to me, but he looked away, pretending not to see me. So I marched across the big empty space between all the Crockett boys and the Pine Haven girls. He tried to duck out of my way, but I grabbed his shirttail.

"Come over here and say hi to me, you little creep."

"Whoever you are, you're not my type." He wriggled away from me, and all the boys around him started laughing.

"Blake, I'm warning you. Mom told me to check up on you."

"Is that your sister? I thought she was just some weird girl," said the boy next to Blake.

"Yeah, that's my sister. And she is a weird girl." Blake walked up and stood inches away from me with a really defiant look on his face. His hair looked like he hadn't shampooed it in three days, but he had a clean shirt on at least.

"How's it going? Are you having a good time? Have you made some friends?"

Blake crossed his arms and tried to stare me down. "Good. Yep. And yep."

"Okay, fine. Just thought I'd say hello." I walked away, but I could tell by the look on his face that he enjoyed this attention and didn't really want me to go. I'd come back and talk to him later when he wasn't being so obnoxious.

I found Sarah and Nicole in the clump of Pine Haven girls still huddled near the screen doors. I waved my hand in front of Sarah's face because she was staring, unblinking, at a spot on the floor.

"I should be boiled in hot oil. Thrown into shark-infested waters. Drawn and quartered." She looked up at Nicole and me with a hopeless expression. "What is drawn and quartered, anyway? I hope it's incredibly painful."

"I'm pretty sure it is. Where's Whitney?" I asked.

Sarah nodded toward the dance floor, and I saw that Whitney was already out there with a boy. "Can you believe how well she dances, considering she has a knife stuck in her back?" asked Sarah.

"Excuse me, but not one person has brought up the fact that Whitney was obviously eavesdropping on us," said Nicole. "She's not totally innocent in this whole thing."

"The only thing she's guilty of is wanting everyone in the cabin to get along and to love camp as much as she does," moaned Sarah.

It made me cringe to think of Whitney just outside the cabin door, listening to everything we said. Had she accidentally overheard us? Or did she stick around, waiting to see if we were going to talk about her after she left? Not that it mattered. What we did was brutal.

Sarah's eyes followed Whitney and her guy. "I can't believe I said those things. I crushed her spirit. Like a grape." Sarah stomped on the floor suddenly, apparently squishing the grape.

"Honestly, she doesn't look that crushed to me," said Nicole. "She'll be fine."

"Stop beating yourself up. We were just as bad as you were," I told Sarah. I thought about how much I'd enjoyed dissing Whitney. It had felt good, in a sick sort of way. It made me feel like I was part of something—a gossip club.

"The thing is, Whitney *is* annoying," Nicole hissed. "Everybody thinks so. Maybe it was good for her to hear us saying stuff that we could never say to her face."

"You're annoying!" Sarah's voice rose with emotion. "Darcy's annoying! I'm annoying! That guy over there in the black 'Rock Star' T-shirt is annoying!" Sarah pointed at the guy and yelled, "Hey, you! Yeah, I'm talking to you. Wipe that annoying look off your face before I do it for you!" When the poor guy realized Sarah was talking to him, his face turned seven different shades of red before he scooted behind a group of boys.

"Sarah, would you get a grip?" I told her, pulling her away. "Look, um . . . there's a way we can fix this. Let's go apologize to Whitney right now." I could do it if Sarah and Nic went with me. But I definitely didn't want to face her alone.

Sarah shook her head adamantly. "No. Absolutely not. I will never be able to face her again. I'm going to go live on the moon. That way I'll never accidentally run into her and have to look her in the eye. I deserve a cold, dark, deserted life."

"This makes no sense to me," Nicole argued. "I can

see why she'd be mad at Darcy and me, but you say mean things to Whitney *all the time*. To her face. She's probably not even mad at you."

"It's not the same! She expects me to mock her to her face. She doesn't expect me to go behind her back and tell other people that she's driving me crazy! Can't you see the difference?"

"Hi, Ugly." Blake had snuck up on us, since we were so totally focused on our girl crisis.

"Who is this hobbit?" Sarah snapped. "Shoo! Go find some dwarves to play with!"

"Sarah, this is my little brother, Blake. Have you danced yet, you little dweeb?"

Blake clutched his throat with his hands and made gagging noises. "You think I'd dance with any of you Pink Haven losers?"

"Hi, Blake. Wow, you sure have gotten cute." Nicole put her arm around Blake's waist. "I'll dance with you, Handsome."

Blake evaporated into thin air. The next time we saw him, he was on the other side of the dining hall, hiding behind a bunch of boys. He obviously knew them. I was glad to see he was making a few friends.

Now Whitney had stopped dancing, and she was standing with Jordan Abernathy and Molly Chapman.

She didn't seem to notice that the three of us were across the dining hall watching her.

"She's probably over there right now, telling them what happened," Nicole speculated. "I bet she'll try to turn the whole camp against us."

Sarah shook her head. "If you believe that, you don't know Whitney." She wrapped her arms around herself, like she was trying to ward off cold weather. She looked like she was on the verge of tears. "Even if I said I was sorry, I still hurt her . . . so *much* . . . I don't think she can ever forgive me. I can't forgive me," Sarah finished off, her voice just above a whisper.

She walked out the door to the porch, leaving Nicole and me standing there.

Nicole let out a long breath. "Wow. I can't believe the drama!"

"Well, we were hoping for a new project. Maybe this is it. Getting Sarah and Whitney back together again."

Nicole raised her eyebrow. "You think? I'd say Humpty Dumpty stands a better chance than those two."

CHAPTER 9

Monday, June 23

"Sarah, you have to come with us," I insisted.

"No, thanks. I'm not going to be good company today. I'll see you guys later."

"Look, Whitney's at her riding lesson, so you wouldn't be going to activities with her now anyway," I reasoned. "If you come with us, we can talk about this and try to come up with a plan." Plans. If we'd ever needed a good one, now was the time.

"Okay, fine." Sarah got up off her bunk and we left together.

"Let's go to Crafts Cabin," I said. "It'll be easy for us to talk there." Sarah didn't say anything, just walked along, staring at the ground. She was totally depressed, worse than I'd ever seen her. She wasn't even cracking jokes anymore.

"Oh no, here comes trouble," said Nicole. I followed her gaze. Mary Claire and her little friend Alyssa had spotted us and were heading in our direction.

"Hi, guys," I said, walking up to them. Nic had said we wouldn't go looking for Mary Claire, but when we saw her, we'd be nice to her. I was going to hold her to that. I introduced them to Sarah, being careful not to mention the word "stepsister."

"We're going to crafts. Where are you guys going?" I asked.

"Archery," said Mary Claire.

"*I'm* going to archery. Spud's just following me." Alyssa peeked out from under her bangs. "Hey, my shoe's untied." She stuck a grubby pink high-top sneaker out, and Mary Claire dropped to her knees to tie it for her.

"Double-knot it. Do the other one too while you're down there."

I glanced at Sarah and Nicole, but they didn't seem to notice what was going on.

If no one else was going to say anything, I would. "Wow, Alyssa. You mean you don't know how to tie your shoes yet? Most kids learn that when they're five." Maybe if I embarrassed her, she'd stop being so obnoxious.

"I know how. But Spud does it for me. She does all my chores."

"Fascinating. Well, see ya later," said Nicole.

I couldn't believe what I'd just heard. "What do you mean, she does all your chores?"

"This girl makes my bed. Does my chores every day. She's not bad to have around. If you can put up with her bad breath." Alyssa smiled, showing off her over-size teeth. It drove me insane the way she called Mary Claire "this girl," like she wasn't even there. That was even worse than "Spud."

I looked at Mary Claire. "You make Alyssa's bed for her? And do her chores for her?" Every morning we all had a chore to do to get the cabin ready for inspection—sweeping, emptying the trash, making sure all the wet towels and swimsuits were hung up. Every cabin had a job chart, and each camper's chore changed from day to day.

Mary Claire shrugged. "I don't mind." She reached for the neck of her T-shirt but then stopped herself.

"And your counselor is okay with that?" I was really fuming now. Sarah was in a trance, staring at the grass. Nicole just stood there with one eyebrow raised, like she couldn't wait to get away.

"She's always in the shower. Anyway, she wouldn't care," said Alyssa.

I stepped up really close to her, trying to intimidate her. "You might not know this, but it's a rule here at Pine Haven that every camper has to make her own bed and do her own chores. If your counselor did find out, she would not be happy. And if Eda, the camp director, finds out, you'll be in big trouble." I tried to sound like an authority figure.

"That's not true." Alyssa stood in front of me with her hands on her hips and shook her head.

"Yes, it is!" I looked at Mary Claire. "Mary Claire, you don't have to do her chores for her, okay? If *this girl* gives you any problems, come to us."

"Bossy Middlers," I heard Alyssa say as we walked off.

"Thanks for backing me up, guys. You were a huge help," I said to the two mutes beside me.

Sarah looked up. "Oh. Sorry. Who were those kids?"

Nicole shot me a quick glance. "The fat one lives in my neighborhood. She's always following me around."

"The fat one? You are so mean," I snapped. "You better not call her that to her face. You'll give her an eating disorder."

"What are you so mad about?" asked Nicole.

"Hello? Did your spaceship just land? Doesn't it make you mad to see your . . . *neighbor* bossed around like that?" I wasn't sure which made me madder—the way that brat had treated Mary Claire or the fact that Nicole didn't even care.

Nicole kept quiet, but I could tell she was offended by the way the corner of her mouth was bent down. Nobody said anything else.

By the time we got to Crafts Cabin, I'd calmed down a little. Gloria Mendoza, the crafts counselor, was busy putting out plastic trays full of fabric strips on all the wooden tables.

"We're making pot holders." Gloria seemed really sweet, with her soft voice and shy smile. She was new this year. New counselors usually got stuck with a boring activity like crafts because no one else wanted it.

"Thanks. We'll work outside," I told her. Crafts Cabin had a porch on the back that overlooked the lake. It was shady and cool out there; plus it would give us privacy while we talked. I carried one of the trays out with us and we sat down on the wooden benches.

"Why did I even come along?" moaned Sarah.

"Have you even tried to talk to Whitney?" I asked. I set the tray on the bench between Nic and me so we could both reach it. She still hadn't said anything.

Sarah shook her head. "I can't." She picked up one of the fabric strips and wrapped it around her thigh, then twisted it like a tourniquet.

I wove a red strip of fabric over and under a row of yellow and green pieces I'd laid out in a crisscross pattern. It was good to have something to do with my hands.

"You know, if Whitney hadn't overheard us, everything would've been fine. Yeah, she was getting on our nerves, but we all like her. And she's your best friend. As mean as it was to say stuff about her behind her back, we weren't trying to hurt her feelings. We were just venting."

Lots of times I'd vented to one friend about another one, and afterward I always felt better. In some ways I thought it was a good thing. Blowing off a little steam about a friend who was bugging me probably kept me from getting really mad at her.

"I know, but she did hear us. And yeah, she can be annoying at times"—Sarah's voice dropped to a whisper, as if Whitney might be lurking under the porch— "but she's such a good sport. She's always put up with me making fun of her. How many people would do that? And she's a sweet girl. If Whitney had been there when we were dissing someone else, I guarantee you she would've told us to stop it."

Nicole gave Sarah a skeptical look. "Wait a second. Whitney was criticizing all the new campers—listing all their problems and saying we needed to fix them."

Sarah let out a low growl and twisted the tourniquet tighter. "It's not the same. She wants everyone to get along. She wants peace, love, and harmony. She's such a good girl!" Sarah wailed. A couple of people sitting inside looked at us through the open door.

"I still say we just apologize to her. We all feel bad about it. We're really and truly sorry. I'm sure she'll forgive us." If Whitney was such a good girl, how could she turn down a sincere apology?

Sarah twisted a piece of fabric between her fingers. "Okay. I'm going to apologize to her. But I want to do it alone. If you guys want to talk to her after, fine. But I think I owe her a private apology first."

Nic and I agreed that that was probably a good idea. I wasn't really looking forward to facing her either, but it was something we needed to do.

"When are you going to do it?" asked Nicole.

"I'll go right now. I'll be waiting for her when she comes back from her riding lesson." She stood up and dropped the fabric pieces back into the tray.

"Good luck," I told her as she walked away.

Nicole waited till she was sure Sarah was gone. "I don't really get why Sarah's so upset. It doesn't even seem like she likes Whitney that much. I always thought she just liked having her around so she could make fun of her."

"Well, I guess that's not all there is to their friendship."

Nicole looked at me. "Are you mad? Because I didn't talk to Mary Claire?"

"No, I'm not *mad,* but I wish you'd stick up for her a little more."

Nic grinned. "Well, I would, but you're a better big sister than I am." She handed me her newly finished pot holder. "I made this for you. A token of our friendship."

I laughed. "How sweet! Guess what? I made you one too!"

CHAPTER 10

Wednesday, June 25

"I hope things go better today with Sarah and Whitney," I told Nicole as we left the cabin for morning activities.

"I'm sure everything will be fine. Sarah's making a bigger deal out of this than it needs to be," said Nic.

Monday after Sarah had left us at Crafts Cabin so determined to apologize to Whitney, I thought we would finally resolve the problem. But she totally chickened out. She told us she'd panicked, that she just couldn't bring herself to face Whitney. This morning Sarah said she was going to try apologizing again at tennis.

Nic and I were on our own for the time being, so we decided to go to the climbing tower.

The climbing tower was gigantic. At the bottom, humongous tree trunks were propped against each other and lashed together at the top with some rope, like a teepee without the skin. Above that were more logs and ropes and a wooden platform at the midway point. Higher up, there was some rope netting that looked like it should be hanging from the crow's nest of some pirate ship. At the very tip-top of the tower was the highest platform, with a roof over the top. I've always wanted a tree house, but our yard didn't have tall enough trees. Getting to the top would be like being in my very own tree house.

"Think I can make it to the top?" I asked Nicole, gazing up at the towering logs and ropes over our heads. So far we'd only made it to the midway point, but I'd always wanted to get to the highest platform, just to see if I could.

"I don't want to go to the top." Nicole frowned.

"You don't have to. You can belay me while I go. Then we'll switch places."

We had to wear safety harnesses when we climbed the tower, and every climber had to have someone on the ground belaying her. The belayer would hold the rope and keep enough slack in the line so the climber could climb easily, and if the climber happened to slip, the belayer would pull up the slack so the climber wouldn't fall very far.

"You look like you're ready for a challenge!" said Rachel, handing me a helmet and helping me step into the harness.

"Yeah, definitely!" I said, although my heart was already pounding like crazy and I hadn't even left the ground yet. "How high is it again to the very top?" I hoped my voice didn't sound as nervous as I felt.

"Fifty feet," Rachel told me, locking the carabiner on my harness to the climbing rope. "But you can practice your climbing skills without going all the way to the top."

Whew. *Fifty feet.* That was so high. I wanted to back out already! "I'm going to the top!" I blurted out. Saying it out loud committed me. Now I had to do it.

Jerry, the hiking guide, heard me say that and grinned. "Sounds good, but just do what you're comfortable with." He was helping Brittany, the chatty girl from the Angelhair Falls hike, into her harness. Erin Harmon was belaying her. Rachel and Jerry stood behind the belayers to facilitate.

"Climbing," I said to Nicole, to let her know I was ready.

"Climb on," she answered.

The climbing tower was similar to climbing walls in some ways. It had the same kinds of holds all up and down the logs.

I was moving along at a pretty good pace in the beginning; the holds were close together, so it was easy to find my handholds first, then my footholds. Little by little, I was working my way up. But it didn't take long until my arms got tired. I stopped to rest and catch my breath.

I made myself look up and plan out the best way to get to the midway platform. The calf muscles in my left leg started quivering from the exertion I was putting them through. I tried not to think about it. I had only a short way to climb until I was high enough to grab the edge of the platform and wriggle myself onto it.

"Great job, ladies!" Jerry shouted from below us.

It felt so incredibly comforting to have something solid underneath me. I sat perched on the platform and peered over the edge at Nicole and the other belayers on the ground. Looking down made my stomach do flip-flops, so instead I looked up at the maze of beams and ropes over my head.

The top was still at least twenty feet above me. I looked up at the highest platform and imagined myself already up there, looking out over the whole camp and the surrounding woods, feeling such a huge sense of accomplishment because I'd made it.

That was a trick Paul had taught Blake and me when

we shot hoops together. He'd tell us to picture the ball swooshing through the net before we made the shot. I wasn't sure if it worked, but it seemed like I'd gotten better lately.

Brittany's head appeared at the edge of the platform, then the rest of her. She pulled herself up so she was sitting beside me. "What a view!" she said when she'd caught her breath.

"I know. Just imagine what it'll be like at the top," I said.

"This is far enough for me. Are you gonna keep going?" she asked.

"I think so. Wish me luck." I looked down at Nicole. "Climbing!" I yelled.

"Climb on," she called back.

I'd never made it this far. I concentrated on finding my foot- and handholds and wouldn't let myself think about how high up I was.

"Up rope," I yelled down to Nicole because there was too much slack. I wanted to be sure that if I did slip, I wouldn't go very far. I felt her take up the slack from below. Then I let go of the pole so I could reach above me for the next handhold.

I'd made it all the way to the spider's web—the rope ladders that would take me up to the highest platform.

It looked like it would be easy to climb, but with every step, the rope webbing swayed, making me feel like I was going to fall right through it. I kept going.

I concentrated on picturing myself at the top, and before I knew it, I was almost there. I pulled myself up and onto the top platform, legs shaking. Far below me I heard everyone burst into cheers and applause. The view was so scary, I couldn't look down. In fact, I wanted to get down as fast as I could.

"Rappelling!" I yelled. Slowly they let out the slack and belayed me down to the bottom.

"You're the first Middler to make it all the way to the top this summer," Rachel announced. Everyone was patting me on the back and congratulating me. My legs wouldn't stop shaking, but other than that I felt great.

Brittany came up and gave me a high five. "Wow, I'm impressed! You got to the top of that thing in no time! Want to give me any pointers?"

I laughed. "Yeah. Rule number one—never look down! But the other thing that helped was staying positive. I kept visualizing myself at the top."

"I wonder if people who break their legs visualize themselves at the hospital," Nicole commented, which got her a few laughs. I knew she thought the whole "positive thinking" theory was ridiculous. Anytime I brought it up to her, she usually made fun of it.

I sat down in the grass next to the belay bench and tried to make my muscles relax. I looked up at Nicole. "Ready to try it? I'll belay you now," I offered.

"No, thanks. I'd never be able to follow in your footsteps," she said.

"Hey, that's not the point," said Jerry cheerfully. "You're supposed to challenge yourself, not try to compete with each other. Just go as far up as you're comfortable with."

But it was obvious that Nic didn't want a turn today. She was ready to leave.

"That was so much fun! I'm really glad we did this. Thanks for coming with me," I said as we walked back toward the cabin.

Nicole didn't say anything at first. Then, after a long pause, she said, "We'll have to do it again. Considering you're such an expert climber." Her voice had an edge to it. The way she said *expert* sounded more like an insult than a compliment.

"Oh, is that what you're mad about? So what? I got to the top before anyone else. It's not like I'm making a big deal out of it."

"You can be a little too competitive sometimes, Darcy. Ya know?"

"What? How am I competitive?" I honestly didn't think of myself as competitive at all. Not with other people, anyway. I only liked to challenge myself.

"Well, you're always saying that you can't believe I get mostly As when you're pretty much a straight-B student," Nic said, conveniently pointing out that she was a better student than I was.

One time I'd made a comment to Nic about how I couldn't believe she got such good grades. Now all of a sudden it was *always*? "Nicole, I *admire* the fact that you make mostly As. I thought A students were a myth that teachers made up to pressure the rest of us."

"Oh, thanks for admiring me."

"What is wrong with you? Are you mad at me about something?" Why did it seem like lately we were on the verge of fighting about really insignificant things?

Nicole snorted. "No! Why do you always think I'm mad?"

"Because you're always so moody. I'm really getting tired of it. What's your problem anyway?"

"Oh, shut up!"

"Fine. I will shut up," I snapped.

Now we were both in a vicious mood. Neither one of us said a word. I didn't even care that she was mad.

I was mad too. I was getting really sick of her constant attitude.

So I decided to pull out the big guns. I had never suggested that we do separate activities because I didn't want Nic to take it the wrong way. Now I was beyond worrying about hurting her feelings. I actually wanted to make her even madder.

"We don't have to spend every waking moment together, you know! It might be a good thing for us to take a break from each other for a while!"

Nicole spun around and glared at me. "That is the best plan you've had all week!"

CHAPTER 11

Neither one of us said another word on our way back to the cabin. We walked in to find Sarah sitting on her bottom bunk.

She took one look at us and asked, "What's wrong?"

"How'd it go with Whitney?" I totally avoided even looking at Nicole. I was still fuming.

"Forget that. What's up with the two of you? You both look like you're ready to scratch someone's eyes out." Sarah looked back and forth between Nic and me.

Nic made a snorting sound. "Nothing that major. We just need a break from each other. *Right?*" She glared at me.

Sarah jumped off her bed, her eyes wide. "Oh, no way! You two can't be fighting! We can only have one war going on in this cabin at a time. What happened?"

I refused to say anything. Let Nic tell her own version of the story. This should be pretty interesting.

But Nic kept quiet too. Finally I started off. "Okay. So we went to the climbing tower, I made it all the way to the top for the first time ever, and Nic got mad at me." I brushed past her and went to sit on my bed. "Sounds pretty ridiculous, doesn't it? You'll have to ask *her* what possible reason she could have for getting mad at me for a thing like that."

I yanked off my sneakers and sweaty socks and tried to toss them toward the spot where all the shoes were lined up on the bottom shelf, but they just banged against the wall and knocked everything out of order.

"Oh, yeah. That's exactly what happened! You totally left out the part where you said I was being mean and you didn't want to hang out with me anymore! Make it sound like it was all *my* fault! Turn Sarah against me too!" Nic was screaming now. I'd seen her mad before, but this was a surprise.

"I never said that!"

Nic growled in frustration. "But you said all that other stuff, didn't you? About how you don't want to be my friend anymore."

I hated that Nic and I were fighting like this, but I couldn't help it. I was still mad. I am not *competitive*. Nic was just jealous because I happened to be good at something she wasn't so great at. If the tables were turned, I knew for a fact that I would've told *her* what a great job she'd done. I was always happy for *her* whenever something good happened. Why couldn't she be the same way for me?

"Hey, stop it!" Sarah warned. "If you two don't stop yelling at each other, I'm gonna bang your heads together like coconuts."

I glanced up at her. "You'll do what?"

"That's what my mom's always threatening to do to my brother and me when we start yelling like this." Sarah came and sat on the end of my cot. "Okay, start at the beginning. Who said what and why?"

I closed my eyes. "Sarah, do you mind just staying out of this?"

"Hey, don't yell at Sarah!" snapped Nic.

"I am *not* yelling at Sarah," I corrected her. "I just don't want to talk about this. If you want to tell her your own fictional version of the story, fine by me." I plopped back on my cot and stared up at the wooden rafters overhead. On the beam right above me, someone had written GOPHER LOVES BEN with a thick black marker. I lay there thinking what a strange message that was.

"Fine. I will." Nic came and sat on her cot. For the

first time all summer, I regretted that our beds were three feet apart. "Here's what really happened, Sarah. We were on our way back from the climbing tower, and for no reason at all, Darcy made this comment about how I was acting totally mean."

She glanced at me and then looked back at Sarah. "Okay, maybe she never said 'mean,' but she implied it. And then she said, 'What's your problem? I think we've been spending way too much time together and we need to take a break from each other.' I mean, that really hurt my feelings!"

I sat up and looked at her. "Nic, I'm sorry. I'm not trying to hurt your feelings. It hurt *my* feelings that you got all mad at me for being good at something. And she called me competitive!" I told Sarah.

"But you know how sometimes you can be——," Nic started to protest.

"Wait a second!" Sarah yelled. "I think I see the problem here. Darcy, you apologize for saying you don't want to hang out with Nicole anymore. You didn't really mean that, did you?"

I sighed. "I said I was sorry five seconds ago, but obviously nobody heard that." I glanced at Nic. "And you know I didn't mean that. Of course I still want to hang out with you."

Nicole looked a little relieved, but then she started yelling again. "No, I didn't know that! How else was I supposed to take that comment? I figured—"

"Hold it!" Sarah raised her hands over her head. "Stop right there. Okay. Now, Nicole—you apologize to Darcy for calling her competitive."

Nicole frowned. "I will, but Darcy, you have to admit that you were making a big deal out of something that's not—"

"Nope! Don't say anything you'll regret. Just apologize," Sarah directed.

"Fine. I'm sorry I called you *competitive*," Nic said with just a slight touch of sarcasm in her voice. It wasn't the best apology I'd ever gotten in my life, but it was better than nothing. I guess.

"Okay. Now you two hug and be best friends again." Sarah stood up and brushed her hands together. "My work here is done."

Neither one of us moved. We just sat on our cots and looked at each other. "You know we never fight," I said finally.

"I know."

"Well, I *am* sorry," I said.

"Me too." This time she sounded like she meant it.

Fighting was weird. When you were in the middle

of it, you always felt like you'd rather swallow broken glass than apologize or admit you did anything wrong. You're always so sure it was the other person's fault. It's like running up against a wall, and you're not going to back down for anything. But then, little by little, the wall starts to crumble.

"See? Now that wasn't so bad, was it?" asked Sarah. She stood there smiling.

"So what happened between you and Whitney?" I asked. "Did you go to tennis together?"

Sarah's smile evaporated. "Uh . . ."

"Uh what? You were supposed to ask her to go play tennis and apologize to her then," I reminded her.

"Yeah, like that's a good idea!" Sarah threw up her hands. "How can you possibly carry on a meaningful conversation with someone when you're on opposite sides of a tennis court!"

"So I take it you didn't go to tennis. Did you at least talk to her?" I asked.

Sarah heaved an exhausted sigh. She refused to make eye contact.

"Okay, then. You settled mine and Nic's fight. Now let's finally take care of this Whitney situation."

Sarah took a couple of steps back. "Just . . . I want to do it my own way."

"Sarah! You're a total hypocrite! Nic and I had a fight that lasted all of ten minutes and you insisted that we make up. I'm gonna go find Whitney right now so we can settle this." I stood up and started to grab my shoes, but Sarah jumped in front of me to block my way.

"Darcy, don't! Please, please just let me handle this by myself." Nic kept quiet and watched us.

"Sarah, today's Wednesday. It's been *days* and you haven't handled it yet. Come on. I really think it'll be easier if Nic and I are with you when you talk to Whitney. You know, you're not the only guilty party here." I looked at Nic for support.

Nic finally spoke up. "If Sarah doesn't want to do it, we shouldn't force her."

I couldn't believe what I was hearing. Obviously, having a referee had really helped us, but now neither one of them was willing to let me do the same thing for Sarah and Whitney. I could totally understand why Sarah was nervous about talking to Whitney, but I thought Nic would back me up on this.

"I swear I'll talk to her soon. Just let me do it alone, okay?" Sarah pleaded.

I let out a sigh. "Well, okay. Anyway, thanks for being here for us."

"Yeah, thanks." Nic looked at me shyly. "You're not still mad, are you?"

"No, of course not. Are you?" We both felt better, but we were still a little shaken up over the fact that we'd had a fight to begin with. It was our first one.

"No. But for a second there, I did wonder if you were going to dump me."

I was shocked to hear her say that. I threw my arm around her shoulder. "Not a chance. BFFs, remember? The second F stands for *forever*."

CHAPTER 12

"Hey, Nic. Are you asleep?" I whispered. In the dark I could see her outline in bed, but I couldn't see her face at all. Lights had been out for almost an hour by my guess, which meant it was probably around eleven o'clock.

"Not yet. What's up?" We had to be really quiet so Libby didn't shush us.

"I just wanted to say one more time that I'm sorry. It was a stupid argument."

I could see Nicole prop herself up on one elbow. "I know. I'm sorry too. But it's not your fault. You were pretty moody today."

We both chuckled softly. I was so glad we'd made up, because there was something I wanted to talk to Nic about.

"I'm worried. I'm having trouble sleeping," I whispered.

"What is it?"

"My dad. His letter about the road trip. Nic, I can't stop thinking about it. You know how he does risky things sometimes? I'm really afraid he's going to get into an accident." Daddy had e-mailed me that day to say he was taking his new Harley on a road trip for a week or so. For some reason, the second I read that, I totally panicked.

He didn't wear a helmet, for one thing. He said he loved the feeling of the wind on his face and in his hair. And he said he wanted to get the new motorcycle on the open road to see how it handled, which I took to mean he was going to see how fast it would go.

"I'm sure he'll be okay," Nic whispered. "You have to trust that he'll be responsible." She reached across the space between our cots and patted my arm.

"That's what I'm worried about. You know that problem he has sometimes." It was a problem my dad used to have, after the divorce. Nicole knew all about it.

"How's that been lately? I thought you said it was getting better."

"It has been. It's been a lot better lately. But I always have this fear it'll come back. You know?"

I heard Nicole sigh. "I know. But if it's been better lately, you have to remind yourself of that. You have to forgive him for past mistakes."

"But why do I feel so scared? When he first told me he'd gotten a motorcycle, I was fine. It surprised me, but I didn't think that much about it. But when I read his e-mail today, it was almost like . . ." I paused, trying to think of how to explain it. "I suddenly imagined him smashed against the asphalt. With his bike all mangled, and . . ." I stopped because my throat felt all constricted and I wasn't sure I could keep talking without sounding like I was going to cry.

Nic waited. When I didn't go on, she said, "You can't think thoughts like that. Whenever you feel that way, just push them out of your head."

"You know what I'm afraid of? I read his letter and I felt scared. What if he's destined to die in a motorcycle accident and I'm getting some psychic message about it? That stuff happens, you know."

"Have you ever known stuff was going to happen before it did?" whispered Nic.

"No. But there's always a first."

"Think positive thoughts. Visualize him being safe. Imagine him having a good time and getting home without even a scratch."

I had to smile over that. I thought it was so sweet that Nic would try to cheer me up with the "positive thoughts" philosophy.

"I know, but . . . I'm obsessing about him having an accident."

"Darcy, I'm not saying an accident couldn't happen—it's just not that likely. Millions of people drive motorcycles every day and don't get into accidents. And even if they do, they're sometimes just minor accidents. My teacher told us he drove a motorcycle from Maine to California when he was in college, and he crashed twice, but he was fine."

"Yeah, but was he wearing a helmet?" I whispered.

"Why don't you write him and tell him you really want him to wear a helmet, that you're worried about him, and that he should do it for you even if he won't do it for himself? Dads love that kind of stuff from daughters."

I thought about that for a second. "Well, I can. But there's no guarantee he'll do it."

I could see Nic sit up in her bed. "What about laws? Some states make you wear a helmet. You could remind him that he might be breaking the law if he goes through certain states."

"That's a great idea!" Immediately I felt a lot better.

I'd write my dad first thing in the morning so the letter could go out in tomorrow's snail mail. "Thanks," I whispered.

"Feel better now?"

"Yeah, tons. You always know how to cheer me up." Ever since our first summer, I'd talked to Nic about all my problems, and it never failed: She'd come up with an idea or say the right thing, and then I'd feel so much better.

A soft breeze came in through the window screens. I could hear crickets and frogs, and somewhere in the trees, a bird was making cooing sounds. I loved so many things about camp, but sleeping with the windows open was high up on the list. At home during the summer we always slept with the air conditioning on.

"What should we do tomorrow?" asked Nic softly. The cabin was so quiet, it sounded like everyone else was asleep.

"I don't care. You pick, since I picked for today."

"You sure we don't need a break from each other?" she whispered.

"I'm positive." Had she really thought I meant that comment seriously? I couldn't believe it when she said she was afraid I was going to dump her. She should know I'd never do that.

"Then let's go to free swim and lie in the inner tubes. And maybe crafts. I know the stuff we make there is lame, but it's fun to just sit on the porch and talk."

"Yeah," I agreed. I imagined what a great day we would have tomorrow, and then I was eager to go to sleep so I could wake up and enjoy it. I was so glad that we'd put that stupid argument behind us.

But there was something that still bothered me, just a tiny bit. Even though Nic had apologized for calling me competitive, she'd never congratulated me about getting to the top of the climbing tower. I was really proud of myself for that. And I couldn't stop thinking about how happy I would've been for her if she'd done something like that.

Oh, well. It didn't matter. We'd both apologized. I knew we couldn't stay mad at each other forever. Even if Sarah hadn't been there, we would've made up on our own eventually. Now all we had to do was make sure Sarah and Whitney worked things out. The one thing a person can't live without is her best friend.

Thursday, June 26

"What would you be doing if you were in school right now?"

Nicole opened her eyes and squinted at me in the sunlight. We were both lounging in inner tubes, our arms and legs draped over the sides, our backs soaking in the cold lake water.

"Hmm, I'm not sure. What time is it?"

"A little after twelve, I think. Would you be at lunch?"

"No, last year we ate lunch at eleven twenty, so we'd be back in class by now. I'd be in social studies. Miss Johnson would be writing notes on the board about Mesopotamia or something. Maybe the Greek myths. We spent a long time on those."

I smiled while I listened to Nic talk. My tube floated gently sideways. The sun made the black rubber so warm that I had to keep splashing cold water on it to cool it off. "I'd be in science right now, probably doing a worksheet. Isn't this better than worksheets and Mesopotamia?"

Nicole closed her eyes and sighed. "You know it."

All of a sudden there was a huge splash that completely soaked us and sent both our inner tubes spinning in crazy circles. When I wiped the water out of my eyes, a wet head came bursting up from under the water and grinned at me. A head with gigantic front teeth.

"Bossy Middlers! Take that!" Alyssa was laughing her head off at the way she'd jumped in and caught us off guard. Squinting, I could see the silhouette of Mary Claire standing by the edge of the lake.

I closed my eyes and rested my head against the edge of the inner tube, like I didn't care. "Oh hi, Alyssa." I waited a few seconds. Then I leaned forward out of the inner tube and tapped her so that her head bobbed underwater.

As soon as Alyssa went under, she popped up again like a cork. "Hey. Cut that out!"

A short toot on a whistle made me look up. Claudia and her friend Shelby stood on the edge of the lake, keeping an eye on the swimmers. "Hey, Darcy. No dunking. I'm not going to make a big deal out of it, but . . . if I don't say something to you, I get yelled at." Claudia shrugged with the same bored expression she always had. She was taking some kind of lifeguarding class, and they had to hang out during free swim and help the swim staff watch over us. Libby stood a few feet away and nodded approvingly.

I smiled back at her. "Okay. Sorry."

Alyssa smacked the water with both hands so a spray of water splashed all over us.

This time Claudia blew her whistle with full force. "No splashing!" she yelled. "Or you'll spend ten minutes sitting out!" Then she gave Nic and me a little wink.

"She's not the boss of us," scoffed Alyssa.

"Oh, yes she is," said Nicole. "They're both training to be lifeguards."

"Huh," said Alyssa.

I looked up to watch Mary Claire still standing on the edge of the lake, delicately sticking her big toe in the water. Then she squatted down and examined the tadpoles swimming around in the shallows. She was wearing a flowered two-piece with a white ruffle across the top and bottom, and her belly was bright pink. I hoped she remembered her sunscreen.

"Aren't you getting in?" I called.

She looked at me and shook her head. "Too cold."

"Come sit in an inner tube. It's nice and warm in the sun," I told her.

"Huh. Spud in an inner tube? That girl will sink it for sure."

I decided my new strategy would be to ignore this little hamster as much as possible. I was glad to see Mary Claire walk over to the pile of inner tubes and grab one. She launched it into the water, hooking her arms around it as she left the lake edge. Her teeth clenched when she hit the cold water, but she kept kicking till she'd joined us in the middle of the shallow end of the lake.

"What's your problem, Spud? Go back and get me one."

Nicole sat up in her inner tube, propping her elbows on the side. "Don't do it, Mary Claire. Make her get her own."

Alyssa pushed wet strands of hair out of her eyes and curled her lip at us. "I'm not getting my own. I'm already in."

"Then I guess you won't have one, will you?" I said. I was so glad that Nic had finally said something to Alyssa. Maybe she was warming up to Mary Claire.

Mary Claire held on to her tube with one hand and

looked at Alyssa. I could tell she just wanted to give it to Alyssa and go get another one for herself.

"Sit it in like this," I told her. "It's more fun this way."

Mary Claire flopped around as she tried to get into her tube. She kept trying to lean back and sit on top of it, but every time she jumped up, she would force the tube away from her. Alyssa laughed hysterically through it all. Finally I held her tube still so she could sit down without it moving.

Alyssa ignored us and practiced handstands under the water. Her skinny little legs swayed back and forth as she tried to keep her balance. I was just glad her head was under water. I liked her much better that way.

"There's a wide-open lake here," Nicole pointed out to Mary Claire. "Feel free to float around wherever you want."

"Okay." Mary Claire continued to float beside us, apparently missing Nicole's hint. Nicole sighed impatiently, but she didn't say anything else. The three of us floated lazily around. Now Alyssa was busy trying to catch tadpoles in her cupped hands. When she didn't have any luck, she went back to practicing handstands.

"You should really put on sunscreen. You're starting to burn," Nic observed.

"Okay."

"Really—you need to remember to do that. It's bad for your skin. Plus it must be pretty painful," she said. "I have some in my cabin if you need to borrow it."

"Okay. Thanks, Nicole." Mary Claire grinned widely, looking absolutely thrilled about Nicole's offer. She kicked her legs playfully and splashed around. It was pretty major for Nicole to even acknowledge that she was alive, much less to be nice to her.

Alyssa's legs fell sideways under water and then she stood up, blowing water and sputtering. "I'm ready to get out. Get my towel for me, Spud."

Mary Claire started to extract herself from her inner tube.

"Don't do it, Mary Claire!" Nicole warned. "She can get her own towel."

Alyssa stood in the shallow water up to her waist, hugging herself. "I'm getting cold. You're almost all dry. Go get my towel!"

Mary Claire bit her lip and looked first at Nicole, then at me. "I think I might stay in for a while. Okay, Alyssa?" she said softly.

"Fine. Stay in here with these bossy Middlers. I don't care if you all freeze." Alyssa splashed Mary Claire just lightly enough that she wouldn't get the whistle blown at her again. Then she paddled to the edge of the lake and got out.

"Good for you. You can't let her boss you around like that," I said.

Mary Claire watched as Alyssa picked up her towel. "Maybe I'd better go. She'll be mad at me."

Nicole grabbed Mary Claire's inner tube and pulled her close. "You can go, but only if you really want to hang out with her. Don't do it just because you think she'll get mad."

"Yeah. If you guys have a good time together and you like being friends, that's great. But from what I've seen, she doesn't treat you very well," I added.

"But she's my best friend. She told me so."

Mary Claire wouldn't take her eyes off Alyssa. I looked over my shoulder and watched Alyssa dry off with her towel. Then she started to walk away, but she stopped when she saw that we were all watching her. Slowly she turned around and went back to the pile of towels lying around on the rocks by the lake edge. She picked up a pink-striped towel, bundled it up, and hurled it into the water, not once taking her eyes off us.

Mary Claire made a little squeak.

"Was that your towel?" I asked.

"That little creep! I'm gonna teach her a lesson!"

Nicole spilled out of her tube and lunged for the side of the lake. I was right behind her. Alyssa was about to walk away, looking extremely satisfied with herself. But lucky for her, Libby got to her before Nicole or I did.

Libby held Alyssa by the shoulder. "Excuse me. Can you tell me what just happened here?" she asked. Libby was amazing. She had a way of talking in this really sweet, calm voice. But behind the sweetness there was something else that let you know she meant business.

Nic and I stood beside them, dripping all over the place. Alyssa stared straight ahead, her eyes two little slants. "I was *trying* to throw my friend her towel. I guess I missed."

"She was mad because she tried to make Mary Claire get her towel for her, Libby," said Nicole. "When Mary Claire wouldn't do it, Alyssa threw her towel in."

Alyssa shook her head slowly, still staring straight ahead. "Not true. These Middlers are known liars."

I could see Libby suck on her lips to keep from smiling. "Well. This is a problem. You say it was an accident— that you were trying to do a nice gesture for a friend. And these *known liars* say you did it intentionally. I tell you what. I think you owe an apology to the girl whose towel got wet—whether it was intentional or not."

For a second it looked like Alyssa wasn't going to

budge. I could see her clamp her jaw shut, and she clutched her own semidry towel to her chest. But after a pause that stretched out for a full minute, she finally looked over her shoulder and bellowed, "Sorry!" at Mary Claire, still floating in the water.

"Okay. Thank you for apologizing. And from now on, remember that it's never a good idea to throw a towel to someone who's still in the water. Wait till she gets out and hand it to her." Libby released Alyssa, who strutted off in a barely contained cloud of rage.

"Can you known liars get that towel out of the lake for me, please?" Libby asked, pointing to the soggy mass floating on the surface.

"That kid's a known brat!" I said.

Libby smiled at us. "Let's just say Juniors have a lot of growing up to do. And you older girls can help them with that." She patted my back before she walked away.

Nicole looked at me and shook her head. "Do you realize Libby just saved that brat's life?"

I laughed. "Yeah, I do." I waded in and pulled out Mary Claire's towel, which now weighed approximately thirty pounds. Mary Claire was busy trying to wrangle all the inner tubes ashore.

"Alyssa's really going to be mad at me now," she said softly.

I wrung her sopping-wet towel out as best as I could. "Are you kidding me? Aren't you mad at her after what she did?"

"Yeah, but if I'd gotten her towel for her, she wouldn't have done that."

"Mary Claire! She treats you like her slave! You needed to stand up to her. Aren't there other girls in your cabin you like?" asked Nicole.

"Not as much as I like Alyssa."

Nicole and I exchanged looks. "Well, think about who else you might hang out with," I suggested. "Of all the Junior girls, I'm sure you'll be able to find a few new friends."

Nic tossed her towel (which was actually one of my towels that she had borrowed) to Mary Claire. "Here ya go. I'm practically dry now anyway."

"Thanks, Nicole! You sure are being nice to me."

Nic nodded knowingly at me. "You think so? Glad you noticed."

CHAPTER 14

When we went back to the cabin to change clothes from free swim, hardly anyone was there. Just Natasha, Ashlin, and Whitney over on Side B. Whitney politely said hello to us, like she always did.

I'd been feeling pretty good about myself since we'd helped Mary Claire stand up for herself. And we'd done it without beating up her little tormentor. But as soon as I saw Whitney, it brought me down a couple of notches.

"We really need to say something to Whitney," I murmured to Nicole as we changed out of our wet swimsuits.

"No! Not without Sarah," Nic whispered back.

"I think we should," I insisted. "We've waited too long." Sarah hadn't talked to Whitney yesterday like she'd promised. Somebody needed to do something.

"Hey, Whitney? Could you come over here for a second?" I called.

Nicole gave me a look that said, *Are you out of your mind?* But I didn't care. Whitney came over to our side of the cabin and stood by Libby's bed, very straight and still, with her hands clasped in front of her. She looked like she was bracing herself for what was next. "Yes?"

"Uh," I began. How was I going to say this? A speeded-up version of our Whitney-dissing played through my head. *Control freak brags too much dump her.* "You remember the dance on Saturday?" I asked weakly.

Whitney remained perfectly still. "Yes."

"Uh. Well. When you walked out, Nic and Sarah and I said some stuff." That was as far as I could go. Nic obviously wasn't going to jump in and take over.

There was a long pause as Whitney waited for me to go on. "Some stuff?" she said finally.

"Yeah. Some really mean stuff. Whitney, we know you heard us. And we all feel really, really, *really* awful. We are so sorry—all of us."

"Do you feel awful because of what you said or awful because I happened to overhear you?" Whitney asked quietly.

Ouch. The truth was, if she hadn't *happened* to over-hear us, then we would've dissed her, laughed about it, and then never given it a second thought.

"We feel awful because of what we said. But we were just being . . ." *cruel, heartless, vicious,* ". . . gossipy, and none of us meant any of it. You know how it is when a bunch of girls get together. One person says something about someone who isn't there and then everyone else starts talking and you're just saying stuff that you never expect will get back to the person, and . . ."

This was not going where I wanted it to go. I looked to Nicole for help, but she just raised her eyebrows at me. I knew what she was thinking—that incredibly annoying people were at constant risk of being ridiculed every time they left a room. She still thought Whitney had brought this all on herself by being so . . . Whitney-ish.

Whitney let out a little impatient sigh. "No, Darcy. I don't know how it is. I make it a practice never to say mean things about other people—ever."

I slumped over and held my head in my hands. "That's a really good practice. One I'm going to follow from now on. Whitney, we are really, really sorry. We said a lot of terrible things, but we didn't mean any of it. I guess we thought we were being funny, but we weren't. We were just being horrible."

Whitney nodded, like she was considering everything I'd said. "I'm curious about something. Today's Thursday. And this happened on Saturday. Why has it taken you *five* days to bring this up?" From the way she said "five," I could tell she'd been counting off every single day that went by without us apologizing to her.

"Well, Nicole can explain that," I said, spiking the ball to her when she totally wasn't ready for it. But why should I be the one doing all the talking? I wasn't the only one who was there.

My comment hit Nic right between the eyes and woke her up from a daydream. "Oh. Uh. We . . . kept wanting to, but we were pretty embarrassed about the whole thing. We didn't really know what to do."

I guessed that was an okay explanation. Not the way I would've put it, but at least I'd made her speak.

"Whitney, we are so sorry! Really, we are. Do you forgive us?"

Whitney pressed her lips together. She seemed to be giving it serious thought, like the decision was a tough one that could go either way.

"Yes, I accept your apologies. I still haven't heard from Sarah about this issue."

"Well, let me tell you—Sarah is absolutely devastated. She feels worse than Nic and me put together."

That didn't really come out sounding right. "She feels absolutely horrible, Whitney! And she's told us what a great friend you are, how sweet and kind you are, and how you'd never treat anyone this way. Which is why she can't even bear to face you. Trust me. This is breaking her heart."

"That's true. Devastated is a good word to describe Sarah right now," added Nicole. "Can't you tell?"

Whitney didn't say anything. We looked up when the screen door opened. Sarah was about to walk in when she saw the three of us inside talking. She did a quick U-turn and started out the door.

"Where do you think you're going? Come back here!" I shouted.

Sarah looked over her shoulder at me. "I'm going to the bathroom. Is that okay with you?"

"No, it's not. I want you to come inside so we can settle this."

Sarah let the door close behind her, and she stood in front of us. No one said a word. Sarah stared at the floor, Whitney looked expectantly at Sarah, and Nic had a strange look on her face—like she was about to burst out laughing.

"Sarah! Say something!" I urged.

Sarah wouldn't look up. "I don't know what to say."

"How can you not know what to say? Why don't you tell me you're sorry?" Whitney blurted out.

Sarah looked at her. "I *am* sorry! I've never been so sorry in my life. I'm the worst person in the world. You have every right to hate me and never speak to me again."

"I don't hate you! But why haven't you talked to me for *five* days?"

Sarah covered her face with her hands. "How could I?"

I looked at Nic and nodded toward the door. Nic followed me outside without a word. We were halfway down Middler Line when she finally spoke up. "What got into you?"

I looked at her. "I don't know. Think I should open my own practice?"

Nic burst out laughing.

"You had the weirdest look on your face—like you thought this whole situation was really funny," I said.

Nic shook her head. "I didn't think it was funny. I just thought it was going to be major drama. Why did you make us leave? I wanted to stay and watch the whole thing."

"I thought they needed to be alone. This is the first time they've spoken to each other in almost a week," I said.

We walked down to the dining hall to wait for lunch to begin.

Half an hour later Whitney and Sarah showed up at Cabin 3's table for lunch, along with the rest of us. They both had red eyes and blotchy faces. Whatever had happened between them, it must have been pretty intense.

After lunch ended, the two of them were walking together through the crowd of people leaving the dining hall. It didn't look like they were going to make a point of filling me in on everything, which I didn't think was very fair, considering I'd played a pretty big role in it all. So I rushed up to them.

"Okay, I hate to be rude, but can't you at least tell me what happened?" I asked.

Whitney smiled at me. "We're friends again!"

"Finally!" I turned to Nic, who'd walked up beside me. "They made up."

"Darcy, you were right. All along, if I had just talked to her, it never would've dragged out for so long. I can't believe I was so stupid," said Sarah.

"You're not stupid!" Whitney protested. "You were just embarrassed. And you avoided the problem instead of facing it and trying to solve it. It's okay, though. We've worked everything out."

Sarah held up her hand like she was taking an oath. "I promise to never, ever talk about people behind their backs, especially my best friend—Whitney Louise Carrington!" She threw her arms around Whitney, and they both got all teary again.

"And I'm going to Sarah's bat mitzvah in November," Whitney announced. "She'll read a whole portion of the Torah out loud. In Hebrew! Isn't that amazing?"

"I am so happy! It's about time you two worked everything out," I said. "I always knew one way or the other, you'd make up somehow."

Nic smiled at them. "I'm glad you guys are friends again. But now what will we do for drama? Maybe Natasha and Ashlin will have a big fight."

"That's a terrible thing to say!" I blurted out. "Do you like seeing people miserable?"

Nicole looked shocked. "It was a joke."

"Was it?" I asked. After all the fighting we'd had in our cabin, how could she possibly hope someone else would have some major friendship war? There was nothing I hated more than having people around me fighting with each other. I didn't get why she seemed to love drama so much.

Nicole rolled her eyes like she couldn't believe my reaction. "Of course. You know I didn't mean it. I'm glad everyone has made up now. Honestly."

I took a deep breath. I didn't want to make a big deal out of nothing. "Okay. No more fights—that's all I'm saying."

"I hear ya," said Sarah.

"Me too," Nicole said, giving me a playful bump with her hip. "We promise that from now on, everyone in Cabin Three will be one big, happy family."

I smiled back at her. "Sounds good to me!"

CHAPTER 15

Friday, June 27

We had just come back from a three-mile hike to Lookout Point. We were hot, exhausted, and dirty, but the hike had been worth it for the great views.

"Thanks for coming with me," I told Nicole. "I know hiking isn't really your absolute favorite activity."

"Well, maybe not my favorite, but it was fun," she said. Lately she'd been a really good sport about doing the stuff I wanted to do. Tomorrow I'd make sure we did something she liked.

We were walking down Middler Line when we saw Claudia heading our way. "Hey! I am so glad I found you. You have a visitor waiting in the cabin for you."

"A visitor?" I asked. "Who is it?"

"She says she's Nicole's neighbor. She's pretty upset

about something. I was just coming to look for you guys."

"Okay, thanks," I said.

Even before we walked in the door, we could hear the sobs through the window screens. We walked in to find Mary Claire all alone in our cabin, sitting on Nicole's bed and crying her eyes out.

"What's wrong?" I asked. Nic and I both sat across from her on my bed.

"Alyssa. She's being so mean to me," she managed to get out between sobs. From the looks of it, she'd been in here crying for a while.

"What's she doing to you now?" asked Nicole.

"Well, she . . . she threw my pillow on the roof of the cabin!" Mary Claire wailed. "And then she said *I* did it—that I was sleepwalking, and that *I* was the one who put it up there! But I know I didn't do it. I don't sleepwalk, do I?" she asked, like she needed Nicole's reassurance to convince herself.

"No, of course you don't sleepwalk. She's just a vicious little brat."

"What did your counselor say about this?" I asked.

"She helped me get my pillow off the roof. She knocked it down with the broom handle."

"Is that all?" I asked. So far I hadn't been too

impressed with the way this particular counselor super-vised her cabin. It seemed like a lot of stuff was going on that she either wasn't aware of or maybe she just didn't care about.

"She told us to be nice to each other and respect other people's property." In between talking to us, Mary Claire sniffled and chewed on the edge of her shirt. It was a weird habit, but it seemed to comfort her a little.

"Like that's going to help," scoffed Nicole. She looked directly at Mary Claire. "You want Darcy and me to take care of this problem for you?" I glanced at her, not sure exactly what she was volunteering me to do.

Mary Claire nodded. She reminded me of a puppy with an old sock in its mouth.

"Okay. We will." Nicole stood up. "Let's go find Alyssa. We'll straighten her out." Her eyes were flashing with anger, and her mouth was set in a thin line.

I didn't move from my spot. "Ah . . . how? What are we going to do?"

"We will teach her the meaning of the word 'respect,'" said Nic, half-jokingly, half-threateningly.

I shook my head. "That won't work. We can't threaten the kid." I thought about all my failed efforts to deal with Alyssa. And how stubborn she'd been with Libby. She wasn't easily ignored or intimidated. That strategy might work with some little kids, but not this one.

"Sure we can!" Nic rubbed her palms together eagerly. Mary Claire had stopped crying and now she sat and watched us, sniffling quietly.

"Look, I'm not saying I wouldn't enjoy throwing *her* on the cabin roof. I just don't think that threats are going to work. We have to think about this—figure out how to get her to be nice for a change."

Nicole rolled her eyes. "There's not an ounce of *nice* in that little monster. She wants to bully someone? Well, bring it on! We'll let her know that she'll get worse than she gives if she doesn't lay off Mary Claire."

"No, if we do that, she'll just . . . dump all of Mary Claire's clothes in the lake. Where's it going to end?" I looked at Mary Claire. "You can't do anything to get back at her. You need to take the high road."

Nicole snorted. "The high road? Where'd you hear that expression?"

I'd heard it from Paul. He used it a lot. Anytime someone honked at him, Blake begged him to give it right back. But Paul wouldn't. *Take the high road*, he'd tell us calmly.

"Everyone's heard that expression." I picked up my pillow and clutched it to my stomach. "If Mary Claire tries to get back at her, or if we do it for her, it'll just make Alyssa that much meaner."

Nic sat down on the bed beside me, obviously disgusted that we weren't going to go threaten a little eight-year-old girl. "We can't let her push Mary Claire around!"

"I know." I had to think about this. "Why were you friends with Alyssa anyway?" I asked.

"Because she's in my cabin. Her bed's above mine."

That whole "you're friends with whoever's nearby" thing again. "That can't be the only reason. Why Alyssa instead of the other girls in your cabin?"

Mary Claire gave this some thought. "Well, Alyssa started talking to me. She asked me what activities I was going to, and then we went together. That's why I liked her. And she liked me because I was nice to her."

Nicole raised her eyebrows. "No. She liked you because she could push you around."

"No, she didn't!" I said suddenly. "She liked *pushing you around*. She didn't like *you*. And she didn't like you because she didn't respect you." I pointed to Nicole. "You're right. Teach her the meaning of the word 'respect'!"

Nic looked at me like I was delirious. "What are you talking about?"

"Think about it! Sure, I would love it if someone jumped every time I snapped my fingers, but I wouldn't really like the person." I turned to Mary Claire. "You think you're being nice to Alyssa when you act like her servant, but then she has no respect for you. You can be nice to her, but don't let her push you around. That's how you'll earn her respect."

"Darcy, can I say something without hurting your feelings?" said Nic.

I looked at her cautiously. "I guess so."

"I know you mean well and everything, but you're not very good at giving people advice. That's really more my department."

"Oh, really?" I tried not to be offended, but that was a pretty blunt thing to say.

"Look, don't get mad. I'm trying to help Mary Claire," said Nicole calmly.

"Well, so am I! What do you think she should do?" I asked helplessly.

"I think *we* ought to let that little munchkin know that if she doesn't leave Mary Claire alone, she'll have to answer to us."

I clenched my teeth. "That won't work! Remember the lake? I think she threw the towel in mostly to get back at us instead of Mary Claire."

"Okay then." Nicole patted Mary Claire's hand. "You be nice to your little friend and all your wildest dreams will come true."

"I could give her my peach cobbler," said Mary Claire.

Nic and I looked at each other, confused by this totally random statement. "Um, okay," I said.

"One time I gave her my peach cobbler. I'm allergic to peaches, so I gave her mine. She was really happy. She didn't expect it."

I smiled. "So she didn't say, 'Hey, Spud. Give me your peach cobbler,' that time, huh?" We all had a laugh over that. "Good idea. Let's think of other things you can do to be nice to her."

"I didn't mind making her bed. I'm taller than she is. She can't reach the top bunk like I can. But then after I helped her, she told me to empty the trash too. That was her job that day. I didn't want to, but I wanted her to like me."

"See, that's the difference! It's okay to be nice to her, but don't let it cross over so that she's using you." I thought about it for a second. "Tomorrow morning, why don't you offer to make her bed? Tell her you want to help her out, since it's harder for her to do it than it is for you. But tell her you won't do any other chores for her. And if she starts being mean, the favors stop."

"Perfect! That'll solve everything," said Nic mockingly.

"Maybe you could pick her some wildflowers . . . or make her something in crafts," I went on, ignoring Nic's remark. I saw my pot holder lying on the shelf beside my bed. "Here. Give her this pot holder. Tell her you made it for her in Crafts Cabin and it's a token of your friendship." I tossed the pot holder to Mary Claire.

"Hey! *I* made that for *you* as a token of *our* friendship. And you just give it away like it means nothing to you." Nic turned her head away and tilted her nose up, trying to snub me, but I could see that she was trying not to laugh.

Mary Claire looked at us. "Okay. I think I remember what to do. One, I'll make her bed. Two, I'll give her my peach cobbler the next time we have it. And three, I'll give her this pot holder. Then she'll like me."

Nicole let out a sputtering laugh. "You do all those things and you'll be BFFs before you know it!" Then I started giggling too. I had to admit, it sounded pretty ridiculous.

"Darcy's Three-Step Guide to Turning All Your Enemies to Friends!" Nic laughed. We were really cracking up now. The sight of Mary Claire sitting there holding my pot holder and watching us just made us laugh even more.

"Should I give her my banana pudding too?" she finally asked. That question made us scream with laughter. I sat up and looked at her, trying to get a grip on myself. Nic was gasping for breath.

"This is what you need to remember. Tell her that you're going to be nice to her, so you expect her to be nice to you. Don't let her boss you around. If she's mean to you, don't do mean things back. And if all else fails, try the banana pudding!"

CHAPTER 16

Monday, June 30

The rising bell hadn't even rung when we heard the knock at the door. Then the screen door was pushed open and Madison Abernathy, one of the CATs, peeked around it. "Darcy Bridges?"

Even though I'd been half-asleep when I heard the knock, hearing my name made me sit bolt upright in bed. Why was Madison coming to our cabin so early, looking for me? "That's me," I managed to squeak.

"You have a phone call in the office." Then Madison closed the door softly, and we could hear her walking back down Middler Line.

My heart stopped beating. My lungs stopped working. I sat in the exact same position, staring at the screen door where Madison's face had been.

Eda, the camp director, told our parents to avoid calling unless there was an emergency. They could write or e-mail us every single day if they wanted to, but phone calls could supposedly make us homesick. In my three years at Pine Haven I'd never once gotten a phone call. Never. I could feel Nicole looking at me from her cot, but I couldn't move.

"Darcy? You'd better hurry, hon. Whoever it is must be waiting on the line." Libby got out of bed and reached for her robe hanging from a hook on the wall.

Sarah sat up and looked around groggily. "What time is it?"

"Seven thirty. You girls stay in bed till the bell rings." Libby came over to my bed. "Are you cold, sweetie? Get dressed and I'll go to the office with you."

I realized I was shaking like crazy. But it wasn't because I was cold. As soon as Madison had said my name, I knew what the phone call was about—my dad.

"Do you have a robe? Can I help you find some clothes?" Libby asked me.

I pulled myself out of bed, feeling wobbly and faint. I couldn't stop shaking. In a daze I managed to find some clothes and put them on. I was on total autopilot.

Everyone was being really quiet. Libby started

toward the door with me. "Can Nic come with me?" I croaked.

"Of course. That's a good idea."

It took Nic five seconds to put her clothes on. Then we were out the door, walking down Middler Line. In the early morning everything felt fresh and cool. Even though I'd grabbed Nic's gray hoodie to put on, I still couldn't stop shaking. Nic hadn't said a word. We just walked briskly along, completely in step. Watching our feet move gave me something to concentrate on.

"It's my dad. He's . . ." I couldn't finish the sentence. He'd never written me back about wearing a helmet. Maybe he didn't get my letter. Maybe I'd sent it too late.

"You don't know that! It could be anything," said Nicole. She put her arm around my shoulders. "Whatever happens, I'm right here."

Now we were walking through the dewy grass on our way to the office. Who would call to give me the news about Daddy? Would it be my mom? Or maybe Grandma? Or possibly even some doctor from a hospital?

Had they called Blake, too? Not yet. They'd call me first since I was the oldest. Then would I have to be the one to tell Blake? If Mom and Daddy were still married, she would be making all the phone calls. But maybe that was my job now.

I realized I was about to live through the worst day of my life. As bad as the divorce was, it was nothing compared to this. And I had one other horrible, selfish thought: If something bad had happened to Daddy, today was my last day of camp.

We walked up the wooden steps to the office. Campers hardly ever came here. It was Eda's territory. The downstairs was the camp office, and Eda's living quarters were above that on the second floor. I knocked on the screen door. Eda appeared instantly, like she was waiting for me.

"Come in. You have a phone call." She was completely calm about it. She didn't want to be the one to tell me.

Nic was about to follow me inside when Eda stopped her. "Why don't you wait out here for her? Give her a little privacy."

I looked at Nic. "Don't move, okay? I want you right here when I get off." I clutched her hand and gave it a tight squeeze.

She squeezed my hand back. "I'm not going anywhere."

Eda took me through the door and into another room. Wood paneling on the walls. Desk. Chairs. Filing cabinets.

"There's the phone, sweetheart. I'll let you talk in private." And then she disappeared.

The phone was an old-fashioned kind with push buttons on the base and a long, twisted cord. The receiver was lying on the desk, waiting for me. I sat down in the rolling chair and picked it up. I could hear my heartbeat pounding deep inside my head behind my eardrums. I propped my elbow on the desk to keep my hand from shaking.

"Hello?"

"Darcy?" Mom's voice said. "Hi, sweet girl!"

"Mom! What's wrong?" Tears were already rolling down my cheeks.

"I have some news for you!" she said in a singsongy voice. "Guess what? I'M PREGNANT!"

A weird, animal-sounding noise came out of my throat, and now I was bawling. "Mom! I thought something terrible had happened! You scared me to death!"

"I took the test this morning! And it came up positive! I ran straight to the computer to send you an e-mail, but then I thought, 'This is too good for an e-mail! This news deserves a phone call.'"

I couldn't stop sobbing. Tears gushed out of my eyes, and my nose was running like a faucet. I had been so terrified. And now I had a gigantic, humongous sense of relief. But it made me even weaker and wobblier than the terror had. I had to prop both elbows on the desk to keep from collapsing in a puddle on the floor.

"So what do you think, sweet girl? Are you excited?"

"Are you kidding? This is the best news I've ever had in my life! I thought someone was calling to tell me Daddy got killed in a motorcycle accident!"

"Oh, honey. A motorcycle accident?"

"Yeah, didn't you know he bought one?" Now that they were divorced, Mom hardly ever knew what Daddy was up to.

"He needs a motorcycle like he needs a hole in his head!" Mom laughed. "I'm sorry I scared you. But isn't it exciting?"

"Are you sure, Mom? The test couldn't be wrong, could it?" When news was too good to be true, it always made me worry a little.

"It was most definitely a plus sign on the tester. I saw it and Paul saw it. Of course I'll go to my doctor ASAP and confirm it. And I've already calculated my due date. It's March seventh."

"When can we find out if it's a girl or a boy?" I asked.

"Not for a while. Do we want to find out ahead of time? I didn't want to know for either you or Blake. I wanted it to be a surprise."

"Yes, we definitely do! Or . . . maybe it would be

fun to wait. Oh, gosh! I don't know! This is so exciting!" And this was just the beginning. I wanted to savor every single second. Years from now I'd be able to tell my little brother or sister about how I was away at camp when I got the great news.

"Mom, is everything going to be okay? I know you and Paul were kinda worried."

"Well, love, my mother and my Nonna both had babies in their forties. We just have to cross our fingers and say our prayers and trust that everything will turn out all right."

I let out a shuddering sob that had been trapped somewhere deep down inside. "Oh, I hope so! I'm going to be a big sister! Again!"

Mom giggled. I could tell by her voice that she was on top of the world. "You want to say hi to Paul?"

"Of course!"

Mom put Paul on. "Hey, Doodle-bug!" Paul always had weird pet names for everyone.

"Hi, Dad!" I shouted at him, and then I felt a little embarrassed. I never called him Dad, but I meant he was about to be a dad. Again. I figured it didn't matter what I called him, considering the circumstances. "Have you smoked any cigars yet?" I added to sort of explain the Dad remark.

"No, but I have been doing cartwheels. Just so you know, I'm pulling for a girl. We need another female in the house to balance things out more, don't you think?"

"Absolutely!" I was secretly pulling for a girl too.

"But don't mention that to Blake. He'll feel outnumbered when Jon and Tony aren't around. And even if it is a girl, remember: You're still my first daughter."

Now I was really sobbing. Before Mom and Paul got married, he'd taken me aside and said, "I don't know anything about raising girls, kiddo. You'll have to help me out." But he'd been a natural. He drove my friends and me to the mall without trying to butt into the conversation, complimented me on my clothes, and talked Mom into getting a cell phone plan that gave me unlimited texting.

Paul and I talked for a few more minutes before he put Mom back on the phone to say good-bye.

"I'm sorry I called so early, but I wanted to catch you before you got busy with your day."

"That's okay! I'm *so* glad you called!" And I was. It had been worth being scared to death. Now I couldn't get over how happy and excited I was. "Are you going to call Blake, too?"

"I'll probably just e-mail him. He's a boy, you know, so I don't think he's going to be nearly as excited as you are. This whole pregnancy thing will be something fun for you and me to share. How's everything else? Are you having a good time?"

"The best! As always! And now it's even better! Maybe this year I won't cry so hard on the last day. Because I'll have something exciting to come home to."

Mom just laughed. "Well, keep having a great time, and I'll keep you posted about all my news. I love you, sweet girl."

"I love you too, Mommy! Bye."

When I hung up the phone, my ear was hot and sore from the receiver pressing against it. My nose was still gushing like a fountain. I raced out of the room and banged open the screen door.

When Nicole saw me, she actually jumped a little. She had this terrified look on her face. "Oh my God, Darcy!" she gasped, seeing my teary face and runny nose.

"No! It's not what you think! That was Mom on the phone! She's pregnant!"

I grabbed Nicole and squeezed her, almost knocking both of us off balance.

Nicole looked completely stunned. "Oh. So it's good news then."

"Yes! She was going to e-mail, but she didn't want to wait. I am so happy!"

"Wow. That's a surprise," said Nic. She still looked kind of numb from the whole thing. She just kept staring at me with enormous eyes. "Why were you crying?"

"Oh, I just got so emotional. You know, one second I think I'm getting the worst news of my life, and then it turned out to be the happiest."

Nic nodded, but she kept quiet. Then we heard the big bell on the dining hall porch clanging, and we looked down to see Eda tugging the rope. That meant it was eight o'clock.

"Whew! I'm still shaking from the scare. Oh my God! I don't know what a heart attack feels like, but I think I had three of them this morning."

"Yeah," Nicole agreed as we walked up the hill toward the cabin.

"You should've heard my mom. She sounded so happy! And Paul said he was doing cartwheels. Her due date is March seventh. How am I ever going to wait nine months for this baby to be born? I'll have to put a new countdown clock on my blog."

Nicole was quiet for a minute. "Then you won't have a countdown clock for camp to start next year."

I laughed, because right now the last thing I was thinking about was camp starting *next* year. "The baby will be born before camp starts next year. First things first. You know what else I want to do? I want to get a notebook at the camp store and start recording every single thing that happens with this pregnancy, starting today."

When we walked into the cabin, everyone was in the middle of doing morning chores for inspection. All eyes turned to me, and everyone paused.

"My mom's having a baby!" I shouted, and then something really amazing happened. Everyone started whooping and shouting and applauding like crazy. They crowded around me and gave me hugs and pats on the back. I almost started crying again.

"Congratulations!" said Patty. "I love babies."

Libby gave me a big hug. "What wonderful news! Be sure to give your mother my best the next time you write to her."

I grinned. "I will. I'm going to write her later today."

"B'sha'ah tovah," said Sarah. "That's Hebrew for 'May the baby be born at a good time, and not in the backseat of the car on the way to the hospital.'"

My mouth fell open. "Really? That's what it means?"

She smiled at me slyly. "More or less."

"I have a nephew, Eli, who's five months old," said Jamie. "My sister sent me some pictures last week—I can't believe how much he's changed since I saw him."

"I wish I lived close to you," said Whitney. "I'd help you babysit."

"Is your mom having any morning sickness yet?" asked Ashlin.

"I don't think so! She just found out this morning."

"Be sure to send all of us announcements when the baby's born," said Natasha. "And pictures."

"I will!" I promised.

We were all chattering away about baby showers, names, and baby clothes. But something didn't seem quite right. Something was missing.

And then I realized what it was.

There was a big, empty, yawning space. Nicole had been really quiet ever since we got back to the cabin. While everyone else congratulated me, wished me happy thoughts, and talked about babies, my Best Friend Forever had not said one single, solitary word.

CHAPTER 17

"Do you see what I see?" asked Nic, nodding at the handful of girls wandering around while we stood in line outside the camp store. "Over there. Mary Claire—in the pale blue T-shirt. She's all by herself."

Small groups of girls were scattered up and down the hill and along the road as they walked to the tennis courts or the lake or the cabins. But when I saw Mary Claire, she was alone. We were far enough away that she didn't notice us, and we couldn't go say hello to her without losing our place in line.

"I guess your advice didn't work. She looks pretty friendless," observed Nicole in a satisfied tone.

"Why are you happy about that?" I asked.

"What makes you think I'm happy about that? I feel

really sorry for her. I should've had a little talk with Alyssa. It was a big mistake to tell her to be friendly to the girl who's making her miserable." Nic followed Mary Claire's aimless walk with her eyes.

"Okay, fine. After we're done here, we'll go find Alyssa and stuff her in her trunk. That'll solve everything."

"There's no reason to get mad," said Nic calmly. "I know you meant well, but you gave her the wrong advice."

"So you've mentioned," I said, shifting my weight from one foot to the other. For some reason Nic had been moody all morning.

"Look," Nic said, "you've said yourself that I give great advice. I've always been able to help my friends with their problems. I practically saved your life our first summer together."

"You did," I admitted. It was something I'd always loved her for, but it was getting annoying to be reminded of it constantly. "I probably should've kept my mouth shut. After all, Mary Claire is *your* 'neighbor,' not mine."

Nicole ignored the neighbor comment. The line inched forward. The camp store was a tiny, one-room building, only big enough for a few people to be inside at one time, and since it was only open during a.m. free time, there was usually a line out the door.

A CAT named Lydia Duncan was behind the counter when Nic and I finally got inside. "Can I have one of those Mead composition notebooks? A yellow one."

Lydia turned to the shelves behind her, which were lined with bars of soap, bottles of shampoo, razors, toothpaste, and Camp Pine Haven T-shirts, sweatshirts, hats, and stationery. "Here you go. Darcy, right? What's your last name again?"

"Bridges—Middler Cabin Three." Lydia nodded and made a note in the ledger to deduct the cost from my account. We didn't have any real cash on us at camp—just an account that our parents had set up for us for little expenses.

"Need anything?" I asked Nic.

"No. I just came along because I didn't have anything better to do."

That comment struck me as slightly strange, but I ignored it. I tried not to stir up trouble by drawing attention to her little sarcastic remarks.

"Mind if we go to the cabin and drop this off?" I asked. "I don't want to have to hold on to it during lunch." I looked around for Mary Claire, but I didn't see her. I was hoping for an update on the Alyssa situation.

"Whatever," said Nic casually. We started up the hill

toward the cabin. "That notebook is just like the one we outlined 'The Plan' in, remember? Only that one was red. Red for romance."

I smiled. "Yeah, I remember." We'd written THE PLAN on one of the blank lines on the front cover.

I'd picked yellow for this one because it was a neutral color for either a boy or a girl. I couldn't wait to write the first entry. *June 30. Mom called me at summer camp this morning to tell me some great news. You are going to be born! We think your birthday will be sometime around March 7. We already love you and you aren't even born yet.*

"What should I write on this cover? I'd like to put 'My Little Sister' or 'My Little Brother,' but I don't know which. I guess I'll put 'Our New Baby.'"

Nic didn't say anything for a while. Then she asked softly, "You really think this is a good idea?"

"What do you mean?"

"You're going to write down everything about your mom's pregnancy, right? Darcy, don't take this the wrong way, but . . . what if something happens?"

I stopped walking and stared at her. "How can you even say that? Take that back right now!"

"Now see—you're getting all upset. I just don't want to see you getting so excited and then if something did go wrong . . ."

"Shut up! Shut up right now!" I screamed at her. I felt like hitting her with my notebook, covering her mouth with my hand, anything to keep her from even suggesting something so horrible.

Nicole sighed. "You are just so emotional about this."

"Of course I'm emotional! Don't you dare ever . . . EVER say anything like that again! I'm really superstitious about stuff like that!" Maybe it was the Italian in me. But I wasn't the only one. At breakfast this morning, when the talk turned to baby showers, Sarah had mentioned that some Jewish people didn't like to have them or to even set up the nursery before the baby was born because they thought it might be bad luck. I felt like Nicole had cursed my mom by even *thinking* those thoughts, much less saying them out loud.

Nic didn't say anything else. My heart was pounding from yelling at her. When we got to the cabin, I put my new notebook on the shelf by my bed. I had wanted to write the first entry right away, but now I didn't really feel like it. I figured I'd wait till rest hour to do it.

Thanks for totally wrecking my mood, I felt like saying. But I didn't. I would try to keep my mouth shut till her moodiness passed.

I just hoped I wouldn't have to wait too long.

CHAPTER 18

Thursday, July 3

I had to admit that the highlight of all my days now came right after lunch when we got our mail. Nic and I checked our cubbies on the way out of the dining hall. Today I had an e-mail from Mom and Paul, a postcard from Daddy, and a letter from Blake.

The postcard from Daddy was a huge relief. It was from North Carolina's Outer Banks, and he said he'd be home after the holiday weekend. And he added, *About the helmet—I got one because I got tired of picking bugs out of my teeth. JK, but when a cricket hits you in the face when you're going 65 mph, it hurts!*

Next I read Blake's letter. He wrote me about the hike he'd been on and how many times he'd done the zip line, and finally in the last sentence he said, *I told*

Mom UR dying to have the new baby share UR room. Ha ha!
He's such a little goof.

Then I read Mom and Paul's e-mail, saving the best
for last. Mom said she wasn't having any morning sickness, but she did eat a bowl of chocolate ice cream with
crushed potato chips sprinkled on top, and she said the
salty/chocolate combo was delicious. She also said Paul
was burning a CD of all his favorite music so he could
start playing it at her belly. And she'd scheduled her first
doctor's appointment for next week.

"You're smiling," said Nic. "It must be more good
news."

"No. It's just a funny story about something the dogs
did," I said, folding up the piece of paper. It had become
really clear in the past few days that Nicole was already
bored with all my talk about the baby. So I figured the
less I brought it up, the better.

"Oh, I thought maybe your family had won the lot-
tery," she said sarcastically. "Something wonderful like
that."

I had no idea how to answer that, so I decided to let
it go. We walked along in silence. "You want to read the
letter I got from my father today?" asked Nic.

"Only if you want me to," I said, feeling a little nervous. If Nic asked to read Mom's e-mail, she'd confront

me about lying to her. Our first summer together, I was always asking her to read my parents' letters and e-mails to help me analyze all the things they were saying. Now we rarely did that.

"Go ahead. You'll see how great my life is." She pushed the letter toward me, so I took it and skimmed through it.

> *Please try to be pleasant for this visit. You seem to enjoy causing conflict with Elizabeth. We will try to have some activities planned for you to do, but we can't spend all our time entertaining you. And no, I can't take time off work while you're here; it's just a matter of bad timing as I'm in the middle of a big project. So come with some books to read and a good attitude. We'd like to enjoy our time with you instead of being in a constant battle.*

"Remember how you told me I should try to spend more time with my dad on this visit? Take walks with him and go out to breakfast? Well, I wrote him and asked if we could take a trip together—maybe go to the beach or something. There's my answer."

"Yikes. I'm really sorry. Maybe he was just in a bad mood when he wrote this. You know—all stressed out from work or something," I suggested, handing the letter back to her.

Nic's dad was really serious and spent all his time at work. I was secretly glad that he and Mom had never hit it off. I couldn't imagine having him for a father.

"No, that's how he always talks," Nic assured me.

She seemed almost glad about it. I knew her home life wasn't the happiest and that she especially hated going to visit her dad, but what I couldn't figure out was why she liked to point out to me how bad her life was and how great mine was. I knew exactly what her dad meant about how she seemed to enjoy causing conflict. I knew how she could be that way sometimes.

"Hey, what if you asked your dad if I could come home from camp with you? Maybe just for a few days." The minute I made the offer, I wished I could take it back. Ordinarily, I'd jump at the chance for Nic and me to be together as much as possible over the summer, but she'd been so moody lately. Plus it would mean I'd have to wait that much longer to see Mom after camp ended.

"You're just saying that because you feel sorry for me. I know you don't really want to visit me at Dad and Elizabeth's."

"That's not true! We could have a lot of fun. It would make your visit with them go by faster. You could at least ask," I said. I tried to act like I really wanted to go home with her. I just felt like I had to do something to cheer her up.

Nic shook her head. "I don't need to ask. I did already. Remember that time you asked if I could come home with you after camp? It gave me the idea, and I wrote my dad way back then and asked him. The answer was no." She looked so depressed it made me feel guilty that I hadn't really wanted to come home with her.

"Well, we'll just have to IM the whole time you're there."

Nicole walked along without looking at me. "So—you got a postcard from your dad, too. How is his road trip going?"

"It sounds like he's having a good time. He did get a helmet, by the way. I am so glad you thought of that. That was a really great idea you had. I would've been a wreck all week if you hadn't talked me through that crisis," I said.

Nic made a little laughing sound in her throat. "Oh, you don't need me anymore. Your life is perfect."

"How can you say that? I'll always need you.

Always! And my life is so *not* perfect. Yeah, we're really happy about the baby and everything, but it's still scary. I mean, Mom's forty-one. She's old to be having a baby. And Paul is forty-seven. Do you realize they'll be in their sixties when the kid graduates from high school?"

I couldn't believe what I was saying. I felt like I was having to look for problems so Nicole would feel better about her own life. And why should I cheer her up by hiding my own happiness?

"Look, you don't have to say those things," said Nic, practically reading my mind. "I can see how happy you are. I think it's great that your mom found someone and stopped chatting with all those sleazy guys on the Internet. At least I'm assuming she doesn't still chat with *Sirluvalot*." Nic glanced at me and snickered. "Remember that picture of him in the Speedo? How gross was that? You think your mom saved it somewhere on her computer?"

I felt suddenly nauseated, like my lunch was going to come up. "Why are you bringing that up now? That was two years ago. Of course she doesn't still chat with any of those guys. All that stopped when she started dating Paul."

One time when I'd snooped around on the computer,

I'd found a folder full of pictures of Mom's online "friends." *Sirluvalot* in a Speedo, lying on a lawn chair. Sickening. Nicole knew how much that bothered me.

"I think it's kind of funny that your mom found your new stepdad on the Internet."

"You swore you'd never tell anyone that," I reminded her, my face feeling hot.

"Don't worry. I never have. I've never told anyone about that or about your dad's drinking problem."

I wanted to grab her and scream in her face, *Are you trying to pick a fight?* But I reminded myself that she was upset about the letter she'd gotten. Maybe bringing up my old family problems would make her feel better about hers.

I took a deep breath. "It's been under control for over a year now. I told you that."

"Well, you mentioned you were worried about him drinking and riding his motorcycle."

I'd never said *drinking*. I always just called it his *problem*. Hearing Nicole say those words out loud—your dad's drinking problem—in broad daylight with other people around made me feel like I was walking through camp completely naked.

Natasha and Ashlin walked past us, laughing about something. "You know I don't like to talk about this with other people around," I reminded Nic.

"Don't worry. They can't hear us. Anyway, I'm happy for you. I'm glad everything in your life is going so well," said Nicole.

"Thanks," I said hoarsely. "And I hope you have a great time at your dad's."

I said it to get back at her for bringing up my family's dark secrets, but she didn't seem to notice. We were at the cabin now and it was time for rest hour, which was a good thing. I didn't want to continue this conversation. My face was still on fire. I knew no one had overheard us, but I couldn't get over hearing her say those things out loud.

I stretched out on my cot and reached for my notebook. Nicole glanced at me from her cot and gave me her annoyed look. I could tell she thought it was stupid that I was writing in this every day. But I didn't care what she thought right now. My pen scratched away on the paper while I wrote down Mom's weird craving for chocolate and salty things. I tried to put an excited look on my face because I knew that would annoy her even more. But I couldn't stop thinking about what she'd brought up.

When Mom and Daddy were going through their divorce, Daddy's drinking was just one more thing for me to stress about. We'd always go out to dinner when Blake and I were with him, and he always ordered a beer, and then another. Then we'd drive home, and I'd watch him carefully to make sure he was driving okay. When we got home, he'd sometimes have another beer while we watched TV.

He never acted drunk, but it worried me. Mom would've told him he didn't need another one, but she wasn't around him anymore. I wondered if that was my job now, but I was afraid to say anything. He only did that right after the divorce, and then I noticed he'd cut back to one beer at a time. Once I even asked him, "How come you never have two beers anymore?"

He'd just patted his belly. "Too many calories. Don't you think I'm getting a little chunky?"

Whatever it was, I was so glad he'd cut back. Nic knew all about this. We had talked about it a lot. She knew how much I worried about it, and how it embarrassed me.

I told myself to just let it go. I knew it had to be hard for her, seeing me so happy about the new baby, knowing that I actually liked my stepfather when she only tolerated Richard, Mary Claire's father, and despised Elizabeth, her dad's wife.

There was a time when we'd shared our family problems the same way we passed clothes back and forth.

Nic seemed to miss those times. In a weird way I did too—a little. It had brought us closer together.

I was glad I had a whole hour to cool off. I couldn't stay mad at her for the remarks she'd made. She needed me now.

CHAPTER 19

Friday, July 4

"They did that in my grandmother's day too. In fact, one year she was the riding counselor who woke everyone up yelling, 'The British are coming! The British are coming!'" said Whitney.

We were talking about one of Pine Haven's Fourth of July traditions. This morning, instead of waking us up with the usual rising bell, one of the riding counselors mounted a horse and raced all through camp doing the whole Paul Revere bit.

"Seriously?" asked Sarah. "That is so cool! Hey, everyone, a hundred years ago today, Whitney's grandmama played Paul Revere on the Fourth!" Sarah announced to everyone sitting nearby. "Only in her day, the rider was naked, right?"

Whitney smacked Sarah with her empty paper plate. "Paul Revere is never naked! That's Lady Godiva. And it was *not* a hundred years ago."

We were all cracking up over this conversation. It was great watching Sarah tease Whitney just like old times. The whole camp had just finished eating a buffet dinner out on the hill, and now we were waiting for it to get dark enough for the fireworks show over the lake to begin.

"My grandmother told me another story about how one year the whole camp was really excited because the new flag with forty-nine stars was coming out—for Alaska. And then the next year, it had fifty stars because Hawaii had just become a state. Do you know that she still has the little flag with forty-nine stars that they gave everyone on that Fourth of July?"

"Okay, now *that* really is cool," admitted Sarah. "A flag with forty-nine stars."

"I know! And just think—my grandmother sat on this very hill, just like we're doing right now, and waved that little flag. Isn't that amazing?"

"Yeah, that is pretty amazing," I agreed. I looked around at all the girls sitting nearby. The sun had already set, and everything was a soft gray. It was easy to let my eyelids droop a little so I wasn't seeing anything very focused. Then I could imagine we were back in time—thirty, forty, even fifty years ago.

How much had really changed at Pine Haven during all that time? We'd often seen old photo albums of girls at the lake or on the porch of Middler Lodge with the backgrounds looking exactly the same as they do now. Only their clothes and hairstyles let you know it was some other time. I looked at the mountains off in the distance and thought about how many hundreds, probably thousands, of girls had sat here on this hill with their friends and looked at the same view.

"Those little Junior girls are waving at us," said Whitney. We looked over and saw Mary Claire with two other girls, sitting nearby. I motioned for them to come to us, but Nicole grabbed my hand.

"Don't bring them over here," she said. "They'll hang out with us all night."

"Oh, is that your neighbor?" asked Sarah.

"Yeah," said Nicole, realizing she wasn't going to be able to ignore Mary Claire. "Darcy, come with me. I'll go say hi, and then she'll leave us alone."

Nic and I brushed the grass off the backs of our legs and went over to where they were sitting. "Hi, Mary Claire. How's it going?" I asked.

"Great! These are my friends—Gracie and Samantha.

They're both in my cabin." The little Junior girls looked up at us and waved. I didn't see Alyssa anywhere.

"Cool. You made some new friends. That's good. Well, we just came over to say hi," said Nicole, hoping we could leave now.

"Hey, guess what? Nobody in our cabin likes Alyssa anymore. She's too mean," said Mary Claire.

"Yeah. We were going to short-sheet her, but we don't know how," said Gracie, the tiny one with red hair and freckles. "Do you know how?" she asked hopefully.

"Well, sort of," I said. Last summer Reb Callison taught me how to short-sheet, but I'd never done it to anyone. It cracked me up to think of these little Junior girls trying to figure out how to do it.

"No, Gracie. If we short-sheet her, then she'll short-sheet us, and then she'll throw all our clothes in the lake and set our beds on fire. Right, Darcy?" Mary Claire looked up at me and smiled.

"She won't set our beds on fire. She doesn't have any matches!" said Samantha.

"Whatever," said Mary Claire. "We just ignore her when she says mean stuff to us. She told me my body odor smells like a goat that died."

"Tell her that a family of beavers wants to adopt her," suggested Nicole.

I poked her in the ribs and shook my head at her, but I had to admit it was a pretty good comeback. "Good plan to ignore her. Well, I think the fireworks are about to start, so we'd better sit down."

Nic and I found a spot in the grass. "Oh, I'm so glad!" I told her. "Mary Claire has Alyssa under control. And she has some new friends! Didn't she look happy?"

"Yeah, she did. You're a great big sister," she said.

"Thanks," I said. But then I looked at her. It was so dark now I couldn't see her expression. Was that a compliment? Or was she being sarcastic?

"So are you, you know. Mary Claire really looks up to you, in case you haven't noticed."

"No, she doesn't. She likes you better than she likes me. Not that I *care*."

Well, maybe she'd like you if you said more than two words to her. "I know you think she's annoying now, but when you're older, maybe you two will be closer."

"Don't count on it. Maybe by then Mom and Richard will be divorced, and he and Mary Claire will be out of my life completely. Nothing lasts forever, you know."

I wasn't sure how to respond to that, so I didn't.

"Well, it looks like your advice worked. *Take the high road.* You should think about starting your own column. You can name it Darcy's High Road."

"Look, they're starting!" I shouted. An explosion of silver sparks appeared over the lake, lighting up the water below. I was so glad to hear the popping sounds of the fireworks. It meant we could put an end to this conversation.

CHAPTER 20

Saturday, July 5

"Guess what? I actually got a semiwarm shower!" announced Sarah as she came in the door. We were all getting ready for the second dance with Camp Crockett.

"How long was your wait?" Patty asked her. "I was in line for twenty minutes."

"Lucky!" said Sarah. "My wait was more like forty-five."

"What are you looking for?" I asked Nicole. She was kneeling in front of her trunk, sorting through all her clothes. All day things had been pretty tense between us, but I was hoping that we could have fun together getting ready for the dance, like we did the last time.

"I can't find my red tank top," she said. "I want to wear it tonight."

As soon as she said that, my heart sank. "Uh, I was wearing it yesterday. Remember?" She knew I'd worn it yesterday—she'd seen me in it. This whole search through the trunk was just an act. It gave her one more reason to be mad at me about something.

Nicole stopped looking through her clothes and glared at me. "I don't remember you asking to borrow it."

I tried to think of the best response to that. *I didn't know the rules had changed. You didn't ask to borrow my white shorts, either. Why are you being so snappy about everything today?*

"I'm sorry. I didn't know you were going to wear it tonight," I said finally. It seemed safer than those other responses.

Nic slammed her trunk shut and went over to her laundry bag hanging on a nail by the wall. The red tank top was wadded up inside. "Great. This is just great. Now I won't be able to wear my own shirt." She pulled it out of the laundry bag and held it up for me to see, like I needed to look at the evidence of my crime. Patty and Sarah glanced at us and looked away.

"Borrow something of mine," I offered. I went to my trunk and opened it up. "Go ahead. Take anything you want."

"I don't want to wear any of your clothes. I want to wear my red tank top."

"I have a white tank top you can borrow," offered Patty.

"Or you can wear this," said Sarah, holding up a red T-shirt. "It might be a little big on you, but you can tuck it in."

"You're all missing the point," Nicole said, tossing the tank top toward the laundry bag. It missed and fell to the floor. "Darcy took my tank top out of my trunk without asking me if she could borrow it."

"I'm sorry. I could . . . wash it out if you want me to," I suggested, knowing that wouldn't be good enough either.

"It'll never dry in time!"

"Nic, please. Can't you find something of mine you'd like to wear?"

"No, I can't! I just wish you'd have a little more respect for my things." She turned her back on me and went back to searching through her trunk.

It would've been so easy to snap back at her, to list the dozens of shirts, shorts, and pieces of jewelry that she'd borrowed from me in the last month. Two days ago she'd worn my pink flip-flops because they matched the shirt she was wearing.

I walked over and picked up the tank top from the floor and dropped it into the laundry bag. "Why are you mad at me?" I asked softly.

"I am not mad!" she said through gritted teeth. "It just annoys me, that's all."

Everything annoys you these days, I wanted to say. But I kept quiet. We all did. Sarah went over to Side B so Whitney could French braid her hair. Natasha and Ashlin came in from the showers. I was glad that other people were around so I didn't have to be alone with Nic when she was in a mood like this.

In my head I did a quick inventory, trying to remember if I had any more of her clothes in my trunk. But if I took them out now and gave them to her, would it make things better or worse?

Nic had picked out a black tank top, and now she was standing in front of the little mirror on the wall, brushing her hair. Then she stopped and went back to her trunk for something.

"Here," she said, approaching me with her hand out. "These are yours. It was really rude of me to keep them for so long." In the palm of her hand were my little heart earrings.

"I don't want them! You keep them," I insisted.

"No, they're yours. I always meant to give them back

to you. I just . . . kept forgetting," she said, her tone not nearly as hostile as it had been five minutes ago.

"I'm giving them to you. As a token of our friendship," I said.

Nicole's hand dropped to her side. She still clutched the earrings in her palm. I watched her expression change a few times as she tried to make up her mind what to do.

"Thanks," she said finally. Then she took the earrings and put them back into the little jewelry box in her trunk.

"I'm really sorry about the tank top," I said.

Nic didn't say anything at first. "Just ask me the next time, okay?" she said finally.

After dinner we had to wait while the CATs and some of the counselors moved all the tables and chairs out of the way for dancing. Some people went back to the cabin for last-minute touch-ups on their hair or makeup. Nic and I waited out on the hill with Sarah and Whitney.

"Is everything all right?" Sarah whispered to me when she got the chance.

I nodded, afraid to say much of anything with Nic around. So I wasn't the only one who'd noticed Nic's snippy mood. I just hoped it would improve once the dance started.

When the counselors opened the dining hall doors, we knew we could go inside. Pretty soon the vans and buses from Camp Crockett were pulling in, and as groups of boys came through the doors, I kept a look-out for Blake. I was really eager to talk to him about Mom being pregnant. He'd barely even mentioned it in his letters, but they did tend to be only three or four sentences long.

"Let me know when you see Blake, okay?" I told Nicole.

"Okay." She seemed to be over the whole tank top incident, but she'd picked one of her own pairs of earrings to wear—some tiny silver loops. I wondered if that meant anything, but I was too busy looking for Blake to really care.

I scanned the crowd of boys pouring through the doors and standing in a clump across the dining hall from us. Not a sign of him.

"He might be hiding from me," I said. "He knows I'll be looking for him."

"I don't see him either," said Nicole.

"There's his counselor in the gray Abercrombie polo," I said, pointing to Brandon. "But where's Blake?"

My eyes kept searching the crowd, but I still couldn't find him.

"Let's go over there and look for him, okay?" I suggested, and Nic followed me across the dining hall. We weaved in and out of the groups of boys standing around, some of them snickering, like they didn't know why we were coming to them.

I was really starting to get frustrated now. I was about to start yelling, "Blake Bridges, where are you?" I was convinced he'd spotted me and was ducking behind his friends, trying to keep out of sight as long as he could.

"Where *is* he?" I asked Nicole. Through the window screens, I could see the trucks and vans parked outside. Nobody else was coming in now.

"I . . . don't see him," said Nic. "I don't think he's here."

"He's gotta be here! Where else would he be?"

"Do you see any of his friends?" Nic asked.

I searched through the crowd, trying to find a familiar-looking face. "I can't really remember what they look like. We barely talked to him at the last dance."

Now I was feeling panicked. It reminded me of the time we'd gone to the state fair a few years ago, and I'd lost him when he needed to go to the bathroom.

"He is *not* here," I told Nic, trying to keep my voice steady. "I have looked at every single boy's face in this room about twenty times. He's not here!"

"Calm down. You said you saw his counselor? Maybe we should ask him," Nic suggested.

I made my way over to where Brandon was standing with a couple of other counselors. Nic was right behind me.

"Hi, Brandon? I'm Blake Bridges's sister," I started off. I was about to go into a long explanation about how I'd been looking for him, but I didn't get very far.

"Oh, hey! Wow, that was quite an injury, huh? Poor kid. Don't worry, though. He'll be out of the hospital tomorrow morning. I'm sure they're giving him the star treatment."

"WHAT?" I yelled.

"Yeah, they'll take care of him. It's really just for observation. He would've been fine in our infirmary, but with a concussion, they always want to keep a close eye on you. I've had two myself—one from football and one from lacrosse."

"*Concussion?* Where's Blake?" I screamed.

Brandon looked surprised by my reaction. "Didn't anyone tell you about the accident?"

"What accident? What happened?"

Nic grabbed my arm and held on to it, maybe to calm me down, maybe to keep me from jumping down Brandon's throat to try to yank this story out of him.

Brandon let out a long, low whistle. "Wow. I figured someone would've contacted you or something. Blake was trying to do a backflip off the diving board this afternoon. He went up, flipped, came down, and smack!" Brandon smacked his hand against his forehead. "His head hit the board, he fell into the water, the lifeguard on duty was, like, *Whoa!* So he jumped in, pulled Blake out, there was blood everywhere— the kid had a gash across his eye a foot long. He passed out cold right there at the lake. It was a major scene." Brandon nodded like he couldn't believe what a great story it was.

Meanwhile I was doubled over, clutching my stomach. I couldn't talk because I couldn't get any air into my lungs. Nic was kind of holding me up so I didn't fall to the floor.

"So a couple of counselors drove him into town to urgent care. He got twelve stitches. By now he's conscious and everything, but his vision's a little blurry from the clonk on the head. So they admitted him to the hospital and they're gonna keep him overnight. They do that when you have a concussion. They have to keep waking you up every hour or so, to keep you from going into a coma."

A little groan came out of my mouth. I leaned against Nic, feeling woozy as an image of Blake covered in blood swam through my head.

A counselor standing next to Brandon smacked his shoulder. "Dude, shut the freak up. She's gonna pass out," I heard him whisper.

"Do my parents know?" I squeaked. Blake was only ten years old. He couldn't pass out, get stitches, and recover from a concussion without Mom there to hold his hand.

"Oh yeah, we called them right away. Don't worry. He's gonna be fine. He really is."

"Are you okay?" the other counselor asked me. "You want a drink of water or something?"

I shook my head. Nic still had me by the arm. "Let's go outside and get some air," she told me. We walked to the door, with me leaning against her.

"I think I'm going to faint," I moaned.

"Seriously?" asked Nic, sounding really concerned. "Want me to get someone?"

"Uh, no. Just let me sit down." We went to the end of the dining hall porch and sat on the steps. I leaned forward, resting my head on my knees.

"Take deep breaths," Nic advised. "Maybe you do need a drink of water."

"No. Ugh. It sounded so horrible—blood, stitches, concussion. And he's all by himself." Then I started to cry. "I wish I could see him!"

Nic patted my back. "Maybe you can. Maybe you could see him tomorrow."

I put my head down and sobbed. I felt so scared and lonely for him. Had he cried? I knew he'd wanted Mom, but all he had were counselors, all those older guys, and he wouldn't want to cry in front of them. And was he really going to be okay? Blurry vision? A foot-long gash across his eye?

"What if he can't see? What if this affects his sight?" I cried.

"It won't! I'm sure he'll be fine," Nic said, rubbing my back.

"I'm so glad you're here. I don't know what I'd do without you," I said.

"I'm right here. I'm not going anywhere," she said.

"Thanks," I whispered, but there was something so familiar about this whole scene that made me feel like I'd done this before, felt this before.

The phone call from my mom. With Nic so supportive and concerned. Until it turned out to be good news. And she'd been mad at me ever since. Mad that I was happy, mad that my life was *perfect*.

"You're a really good friend," I managed to say through my tears. *As long as there's a crisis.*

"Thanks." She patted my back. But now her pats annoyed me and I wanted to push her hand away. But I didn't. I just cried and cried and cried.

Mostly I cried for Blake. But there was another reason. I had a horrible, sick feeling that deep down in some secret part of herself that she would never admit to, Nicole was enjoying this.

CHAPTER 21

Sunday, July 6

That night I fell into a half sleep that lasted all night long. I drifted in and out of dreams, rolled over and over trying to find a comfortable spot, and dozed off only to jerk myself awake for no apparent reason.

Mostly I kept thinking about Blake, lying in a hospital bed, his head bandaged. But there was something else that kept swimming around inside my head every time I started to drift off to sleep.

I'm right here. I'm not going anywhere.

Nicole had been a great friend, my *best* friend, the one I could talk to about anything. The one who'd helped me live through my parents' divorce, the one who could always give me advice when I had a problem.

But this summer, we'd fought more than ever. Well,

not exactly fought. It was just that she'd often been annoyed about something or other. And this last week especially, I'd felt like I had to hide my happiness from her, that I couldn't talk to her about how excited I was about the new baby without her getting all quiet and moody. But the second there was a problem, she was right by my side.

I rolled over and looked at the dark outline of Nicole in her cot. She was asleep; everyone was asleep. It was probably about two or three o'clock in the morning.

Something was not right. What kind of friend gets mad at you when you're happy, and enjoys it when you're having a crisis?

It wasn't that she was cruel. She wasn't *glad* that Blake had gotten hurt. But she did seem to enjoy being the one to give everyone advice, to help people with their problems. She wanted to be the shoulder to lean on.

Which was fine, really. I really had needed her tonight. But if she wanted to help me through the bad times, why couldn't she be happy for me during the good times?

I looked at the dark lump in the cot next to me. I was tempted to wake her up right now and confront her. *What's wrong with you? Can you only be my friend when I'm unhappy?*

I decided I had better get some sleep.

Finally, sometime in the early morning hours, I did fall asleep. But when the rising bell rang, I could barely open my eyes. I stayed in bed, not moving, for as long as I could. I remembered it was Sunday, and that meant we didn't have to clean the cabin for inspection, and we could go to breakfast in pajamas. I rolled over and buried my face in my pillow while everyone else got out of bed. A hot feeling was burning deep inside my stomach.

I felt a hand patting my back. I opened one eye to see who it was. Nic, of course. My *best* friend. The feeling got hotter.

"Time to get up," she said softly. I could hear the screen door opening and closing as everyone else left the cabin. I sat up so Libby would know I was awake.

"You feel okay?" asked Nicole, looking concerned.

"No. I feel horrible," I told her.

"Well, don't worry. Maybe you can talk to Eda about what happened. Maybe they'll let you go see Blake today. I'll go with you. To talk to her, I mean. And to go see him too—that is, if you want me to."

I stood up and slipped my feet into my flip-flops. I was cold with just a cami and pajama pants on, but I didn't bother to put my robe on. Every muscle in my body felt tense and ready to snap. The cabin was almost empty, except for Claudia and Jamie still over on Side B. I waited till they had walked out the door before I looked at Nicole.

"You'd like that, wouldn't you?"

A look of surprise spread across her face. "Like what?"

"To go with me and see Blake all bandaged up. Whenever I have a problem, you're right by my side, aren't you?"

Nic stared at me, her mouth slightly open.

"But if it's good news, if I'm happy about something, you can't stand that, can you?" *I should stop*, I thought. *I should walk out the door now. Go to the bathroom, the dining hall. Go somewhere where I won't be able to say these things.*

Nic cleared her throat. "You're my best friend. Of course I want you to be happy." Her voice sounded raspy, like somebody else's.

"Do you? Do you really? Because it sure seems like anytime things are going good for me, you get mad about it. There's something really twisted about a friend who only likes you when you're having problems."

Nicole was absolutely still, absolutely quiet. "Twisted," she said finally. It felt like a Ping-Pong ball that I'd slammed across the table at her, and now she was tapping it back to me, waiting to see what I would do with it.

I should take it back. Cup it in my hand and never let her see it again. Tell her I didn't mean it that way. But I did mean it. It was true. I remembered the look on her face when I told her Mom was pregnant. And the look she got every time I mentioned the baby or reached for my journal.

I should say something else. Explain the horrible, overtired feeling that the sleepless night had left me with. Tell her that I *did* want her to always be the one standing outside the door waiting if there was ever a frightening phone call. But there was something else I wanted to say to her.

Pretend you're happy for me! Even if you're so jealous of my life that you can't hide it.

"I'm sorry," I finally said.

But it was too late. Nicole had already walked out the door.

CHAPTER 22

"He looks fine. Way better than I was expecting," I told Mom.

"What about the scar? How bad is that going to look?" she asked.

"Well, it looks pretty bad now—like Frankenstein. It's long. It's above his right eye. But if he lets his hair grow, it'll cover it." The scar was maybe two inches long, not a foot, like Brandon had said. But it did look really big the way it cut across his forehead.

"Are you sure he's okay? Maybe we should come and get him—bring him home early."

"Mom, honestly, I'd be the first to tell you if I thought you should do that. But you should see him. He looks like they pinned a medal on him or something. He's loving every minute of this."

Blake grinned at me when he heard that.

"Mom wants to say good-bye to you," I said, handing him the phone. He sat up in bed, taking the receiver from me.

"NO! Do not come and get me! I have a whole week left! I'd miss everything!" he screamed.

"Calm down. You'll bust a stitch," I whispered to him, patting his legs through the blanket.

"Okay. Love you, too. Bye." He hung up before I got a chance to talk to Mom about how she was feeling. He picked up the hand mirror lying beside him and looked into it for about the fortieth time since I'd walked in.

"It's so cool, isn't it? It looks like I was in a wicked fight," he said, examining the neat row of stitches across his forehead. He had a black eye, too, but the nurse said that was normal with a head injury.

"Yeah, it really does. Are you sure your head doesn't hurt?"

"A little, but the nurse gave me some Motrin about an hour ago. I hope I don't have to spend the night here," he said. When they'd released him from the hospital this morning, the counselors had brought him to the Camp

Crockett infirmary. His concussion was a mild one, but they still wanted to make sure he got plenty of rest.

"And no more blurry vision? How many fingers am I holding up?" I held up two fingers on one hand and three on the other.

"Thirty-seven. When Rob drove me back from the hospital this morning, we stopped at Sonic, and I got a corn dog, a large order of onion rings, and a chocolate shake. He paid for it with his own money, too."

"Oh, that explains your stinky breath! I'm glad they're taking good care of you."

The nurse came in and smiled at Blake. "Do you think you're up for a few more visitors?" she asked.

"Yeah! Definitely!" said Blake. Five boys came pouring into the room, and they were all giving him high fives and oohing and aahing over his stitches.

"Sick! You look so cool!"

"Dude—you got a black eye and everything!"

"Brandon said your brain was oozing out. Did they shove it back in or what?"

I have never seen Blake happier than when he had all his friends crowded around him, admiring his wounds. A couple of them had cameras so they could take his picture. Then he told them the story of how his head had hit the board, slapping his hands together to make the sound effects and snapping his head back to show the impact. The nurse only let them stay about fifteen minutes before she made them leave.

"I should probably go too," I told him. "Oh, by the way, Mom and Paul said they were going to GameStop for *something*, so you might ask them about that when they pick us up on Saturday." Saturday—it was hard to believe camp would be over in a week.

"Cool. Thanks for coming to see me." He let me hug him before I left. I was really glad I'd had the chance to see him with my own eyes, and to talk to Mom. I felt so much better now.

Libby was waiting outside on the infirmary porch, talking to the nurse. "How is he?" she asked.

"He's great. He's an instant celebrity now."

The nurse assured me she'd keep a close eye on him for the rest of the week, and then Libby and I left. On the drive back to Pine Haven, Libby asked me all about Mom and kept the conversation focused on the new baby, maybe to take my mind off Blake's injury. But all I could think about was what I was going to say to Nicole when I got back to camp. I never should've said those things this morning.

"Okay. It's ten after five. I'm going to rush off to the staff meeting, but I'll see you later at dinner, all right?" said Libby as we pulled into camp.

"Sure. Thanks so much for going with me to talk to Eda. And for taking me over there. If I hadn't had a chance to see him, I would've worried about him all week," I told Libby.

We said good-bye, and she went off to Senior Lodge to meet with the other counselors for the weekly staff meeting. Now was the perfect time to talk to Nicole; we had about an hour before dinner. Maybe we could go out on the hill so we'd have some privacy.

I knew exactly how I'd start the conversation off—by telling her that she was the best friend I'd ever had, that I never could've lived without her the past two years, and that I wanted to share everything with her— clothes, jewelry, good news . . . whatever. We only had a week of camp left, and I wanted it to be a good one.

As I got to the cabin, I could hear voices inside. Nic's voice. "I'm sick of this! *Oh, we're so worried about Darcy. I hope her brother's okay. I hope her mom has twins.* Well, I've got news for you. This morning, when I was trying to cheer her up about her brother, she called me *twisted.* And I'm supposed to be her best friend."

I stood paralyzed by the side of the cabin. Frozen. Not breathing. Not moving.

"Give her a break. She was upset." That was Sarah.

"Oh, so if she's upset, she can say whatever she wants

to me. Everyone thinks Darcy's this sweet little angel."
Nic's voice had that edge to it. I knew that tone. "If only
you guys knew how screwed up her life really is."

"You need to stop talking." That was Sarah again.

"I agree. It's completely . . ." something I couldn't
hear. Whitney's voice. So she was in there too.

"You want to talk about inappropriate? Her new
stepfather, the one her mom's having the baby with—
you want to know how they met? There were all these
random guys that her mom picked up off the Internet.
Darcy was so freaked out by it. Her mom would spend
hours and hours online, chatting with these guys. That's
why Darcy's dad divorced her."

That wasn't even true! This was not happening. I was
dreaming this.

There was a thump, like somebody threw something.
Maybe a pillow.

"Don't throw things at me, Sarah!" yelled Nicole.

"Then shut up, Nicole! We don't want to hear this!"

"Everyone needs to calm down." That sounded like
Claudia. *Was the whole cabin listening to all this?*

"You all have this image of who Darcy is, but you
don't know her the way I do. Her family has all kinds of
issues, even though she tries to hide it. Her father's an
alcoholic, but she won't admit to it."

Then I could move again. Instantly, I was inside the cabin somehow.

"She's lying." I looked straight at Nicole. "That's a lie. Tell them you're lying."

CHAPTER 23

The strange thing was how calm I felt. Sarah, Whitney, Claudia, and Patty were all inside, all with the exact same expression on their faces when the door opened. Shock.

Nicole was the only one who didn't look that surprised to see me. A little at first when I walked in the door. But she got over it pretty fast. She tensed her jaw and looked right at me. Sarah closed her eyes and covered her face with her hands. She didn't want any part of this.

"She's lying. My father's not an alcoholic."

Sarah shook her head. "Let's not even go there."

"Good idea," agreed Patty. It was the first time I'd heard her speak up.

Nicole's eyes bored into mine. She wasn't backing off at all. I knew she wouldn't.

"I heard it all. Or a lot of it." Still so calm. I hadn't even raised my voice. I'd never been this calm in my life.

"So you were eavesdropping," said Nic, nodding. Like she expected that, like it was no surprise that I'd stoop that low.

"No. Not at all. Step outside. You'd be surprised how well you can hear everything through those screens."

"I have an idea. Let's all forget this ever happened," Sarah suggested.

"You want me to forget this ever happened?" I asked Nicole. We were the only two people in the room now. Everyone else had faded away. I couldn't even see them or remember exactly who they were.

"It's not a lie, and you know it." Nic challenged me to deny it.

Parts of it were true. Mom chatting with strange men—true. Daddy divorcing her because of it—not true. Daddy drinking too much at times—true. Alcoholic—not true. Partly the truth, but twisted to make things sound a little bit worse than they were. *Twisted.*

"I know the truth, and you know the truth," I said to her. "As long as we're telling the truth, why don't you tell everyone about *your* family and all *your* issues." Now, for the first time, Nicole did look concerned. I'd struck gold.

"Why don't you tell them about how both your parents got restraining orders against each other during their divorce? And how many times the police were called to break up their fights and how you'd hide under your bed when that happened?"

Nicole swallowed once. Her eyes were locked on mine and she couldn't look away. Somebody said something, but I didn't hear it. I couldn't hear anything over the sound of my own voice.

"And your own father doesn't even remember your birthday. How last year you waited and waited for him to call you, but he never did, and then four days later when he finally did remember, he called and yelled at you. And he blamed you for not reminding him. And how your very own stepsister goes to this camp, but you pretend you don't even know her. Mary Claire Mitchell—that little Junior who's always hanging around. Your *sister*, not your neighbor. Your family's so screwed up, you act like they don't even exist."

Sarah was standing in between us. "Both of you need to stop talking." She held her hands up like she needed to hold us back from each other, in case things got physical.

But it wasn't like that at all. We just stared at each other, daring the other one to look away. Neither one of us would.

Whitney stepped in. "Okay, people say things when they're angry, but it doesn't . . . you should . . ." Things must be bad if even Whitney was at a loss for words.

Then Libby and Jamie walked in the door, and they both came to a dead stop when they saw the looks on everyone's faces.

"What's going on? What's wrong?" asked Libby.

I unlocked my eyes from Nicole's and turned toward Libby. "Nothing. We were just talking."

CHAPTER 24

Tuesday, July 8

I tapped softly on the screen door in case somebody was inside. When I didn't hear anything, I opened the door and stepped in. The cabin was empty. Everyone was at activities.

Strange. Everything looked so different. If I didn't know this was Cabin 4 from the number on the door, I would think I was in the wrong cabin. The first thing I noticed was that the two sets of bunk beds on Side B weren't there. Now there were two singles and one set of bunk beds. I stood still for a few minutes, looking around. Then I tiptoed over to Side B.

I wasn't sure why I was being so quiet. I didn't need to be. Maybe because I was trespassing, in a way. This wasn't my cabin anymore. If any of the Cabin 4 girls walked in, they'd be surprised to see me, just like I'd be surprised to come home and find one of my neighbors snooping around in my house.

One of the single cots was pushed up against the wall—that was the spot I wanted to look at. I stood in front of the bed, leaning over so I could look at the wall. I didn't want to sit on whoever's bed this was with the yellow sheets and the purple cotton blanket.

Where was it? It had to be here someplace. It should be right here. But I couldn't find it. Last year our bunk beds had been against this wall. I knew this had to be the right spot. I was about to go ahead and sit on the bed so I could see better, but then I looked a little higher, and there it was. It was higher up than I remembered it.

DARCY AND NICOLE, written with a red Sharpie. Then under it, BEST FRIENDS FOREVER!!! Nic had been the one to write three exclamation marks. And the date. JULY 5. One year and three days ago. But it seemed longer.

We'd sat on Nic's bottom bunk to write it—Nic's bed with the pink-and-red polka-dot sheets—the same sheets that were on her bed right now in Cabin 3. It was right after dinner and everyone was leaving for evening program. We were the only ones in the cabin, and we'd decided we'd better sign the wall while we had a chance. We didn't want to wait till the last day of camp, when we'd be all sad and depressed.

I reached out and touched the rough wood. I wondered if any of this year's Cabin 4 girls had read this. So far this year, I hadn't gotten around to writing my name anywhere. It had seemed like I had plenty of time to do it.

I stood there and looked at the wall for a long time. I kept thinking I should leave, in case anyone walked in. If anyone did, I could easily explain why I was here—I'd just come by to find where I'd signed my name last year. No big deal. They wouldn't care. Graffiti covered the walls of all the cabins. Everyone signed her name somewhere.

Eventually I went back to my own cabin—Cabin 3. It was empty too. All summer long I had barely had a single moment by myself. And I wouldn't be alone now if I'd gone to afternoon activities like I was supposed to.

I sat on Nic's cot instead of mine, for some reason. I didn't really know why. Her bed was neatly made, with her pink blanket folded down so you could see the polka-dot sheets.

What if. What if I'd come back one minute earlier or one minute later Sunday, and I hadn't overheard Nic talking? But if I was going to play that game, I could say what if I hadn't called Nic twisted, what if I'd slept better Saturday night, what if Blake had sprung up two inches higher and hadn't hit his head at all?

Would we still have had this fight?

Mom believes in destiny. She thinks everything happens for a reason. One time she told me that she really believed the only reason she had married Daddy was because Blake and I needed to be born, and that once that was taken care of, they were supposed to go their separate ways. At the time I didn't believe that; I was still hoping they'd work things out and stay together. But now I have to admit that everyone is a lot happier.

But why had destiny made our family happy when Nic's family still had problems? It was like they'd traded one set of problems for another. That didn't seem fair. I'm sure Nic wondered, *Why is Darcy's life turning out so great when mine is still a mess?* I couldn't blame her for thinking that. I would too, if I were in her shoes.

The screen door opened, and Sarah and Whitney came in.

"Hi," said Sarah. She glanced at my empty bed and then back at me sitting on Nicole's bed. "We've been looking for you."

"You found me."

Whitney came over and sat on my bed. Sarah took

a seat beside her. "Darcy, you've both had a chance to cool down a little. Now it's time for you to talk to each other," said Whitney.

I shook my head.

"Don't try to get out of it! We're staging an intervention," said Sarah.

It was so easy to tell everyone else what to do. *Go apologize. Just talk to her. Everything will work out.* I never once thought about how Sarah felt, or how Whitney felt. All the hurt feelings, the anger, the embarrassment. I didn't think about how that all got in the way and made everything so much harder.

I knew we should talk. I just didn't want to. And Nicole didn't either. It felt better to just avoid each other as much as possible.

"We've looked all over for Nicole, but we can't find her," said Whitney. "She'll have to show up for dinner, and before evening program tonight Sarah and I are going to sit the two of you down and make you talk about this. I know neither one of you really wanted this to happen."

That sounded odd. Of course we didn't want to have a big fight.

Or did we? It seemed like for days before it happened, Nic had been pushing me. Almost trying to make me mad. But why? Why was she mad at me? And I'd gotten fed up too. I was the one who started it by calling her twisted. Or did she start it with the argument over the tank top? But even before that, she'd said those things about maybe Mom having problems with her pregnancy. It was hard to trace back when exactly things started falling apart.

"Thanks, guys. I know you're trying to help. But I really don't want to talk to her. Yet. Maybe later."

"No, not later. Today. You have to," said Sarah. "We'll be there with you if you want us to. Or we'll leave you alone. Whatever. But you guys can't go another night without speaking to each other."

"Maybe," I said.

If Nic and I were forced to sit down and apologize, there was a chance everything could somehow be okay. The way I felt now, it didn't seem like it could work out, but it might. Maybe she'd be the old Nic, the one who wasn't always annoyed with me about something, the one who I could talk to in ways I couldn't talk to anyone else.

But when we all went to dinner, Nic wasn't there. I waited for Libby or Jamie to ask about her, but neither of them did. They started passing around plates and food dishes like nothing was out of the ordinary at all.

"Where's Nicole?" Sarah finally asked .

"Oh, she went to the infirmary," said Libby. "After rest hour she told me she wasn't feeling well. I guess she's come down with that virus that's been going around."

Sarah and Whitney looked at me. I could tell they were wondering what I was wondering—was Nicole really sick, or was she just avoiding me? She might really and truly be sick. Because I knew one thing—I'd never felt so bad in all my life.

CHAPTER 25

Wednesday, July 9

Late in the afternoon, after activities were over, Nic came back. I looked up when she walked in the cabin door. Natasha and Ashlin were over on Side B, but everyone else was off someplace, doing other things.

"Hi," I said. It was the first word I'd said to her since Sunday evening.

"Hi," she answered. She dropped a plastic bag of clothes on her bed.

"How do you feel?" I asked.

"Better. My fever's gone, anyway."

"You had a fever?" I asked. I guess she really was sick. Or maybe she'd made it up to make it sound better.

"Yeah. Not a high one—100.2. Where's Sarah?"

"She's with Whitney. Whitney's practicing for the

talent show. She's going to play the violin. It's tomorrow night, you know."

"Oh, yeah." Nic smiled a little. "Well, with Whitney doing an act, Cabin Three is bound to win."

Nic looked at the bag of clothes on the bed. "Libby brought me some stuff—my toothbrush and some clothes. That's your Pine Haven T-shirt," she said, nodding to the green shirt that had spilled out of the plastic bag onto the bed. "I guess it was in my trunk. I wore it because that's the only shirt she brought me." She picked up the shirt and handed it to me.

"I'm glad you're feeling better."

Nic looked out the screen window. "I thought *maybe* you would've come to see me."

I'd thought about it. Part of me wanted to go to the infirmary and check on her. But part of me was glad we didn't have to face each other. And I was sort of afraid to go. I imagined going to the nurse and asking to see Nicole, only to hear her voice yelling from some far-off corner, *Tell her to go away! Tell her I never want to see her again!*

"I wasn't sure . . . if you could have visitors," I said finally.

"You went across town to see Blake," said Nic, still looking out the window. She was watching a red bird on a branch right by the windowsill.

"He's my brother," I said, and the second I said that, I knew it was the wrong thing to say. But I couldn't take it back. I'd never be able to make it sound right. "I missed you, though," I added.

"Did you?"

"Yeah. I really did." *I still do.*

Nic didn't say anything for a long time. "Well, that's something at least."

I sat cross-legged on my bed, my elbows propped on my knees, staring down at my green Pine Haven shirt in my lap. "I wish I could rewind everything and go back to . . ." To when? When would I like to turn things back to? To the last time we'd really had a good time together. Whenever that was. Was it the first dance when we picked out clothes together? It hadn't been *that* far back, had it? "I'm sorry I called you twisted. I didn't mean it. I was just so tired that morning. And worried about Blake."

Nic had a strange smile on her face. "You know what I find the most interesting about all this?" she asked, turning away from the red bird to look at me.

"What?" I felt a tightness in my stomach, like I needed to brace myself.

"You said every mean thing you could think of—that stuff about my birthday, the restraining orders, Mary

Claire. You sure didn't hold back." Nic turned back to the window, but the red bird was gone now. "So much for the high road."

I could solve lots of people's problems by sitting back and watching and saying, *This is what should happen.* That was the easy part. It ended up being a lot harder to take the high road than I thought it was.

"I know, I know. I wanted to get back at you. For telling everyone my father was an alcoholic. You know he's not."

"You've said yourself that you think he might have a drinking problem. That you always have to watch him and count how many beers he has and make sure he's okay to drive. I didn't make that stuff up!" said Nicole, her voice rising with emotion.

"I told you it was better! It hasn't been like that for almost two years!" Why were we arguing about this, anyway? This wasn't what the fight was about.

Ashlin and Natasha left the cabin. They were the only ones who'd missed the big scene on Sunday, but no doubt everyone else had filled them in about it.

"I'm sorry I said all those things," I told Nicole. "I wish I could take everything back. I just want things to be normal again."

Nicole kept quiet. "Yeah. Me too," she said at last.

What did that mean? That she was sorry too? That she was taking everything back too?

"I can't stand it when we're fighting. We never used to fight."

Nic nodded. "I know. This was my worst fear. I've always been afraid this would happen."

"What?" I asked. I had no idea what she was talking about.

"That one day you'd dump me," she said very quietly. She wouldn't look at me.

"How can you say that?" I practically shouted. "Remember all those times when we said we'd be counselors together, and then we'd be college roommates? We were even going to share an apartment together one day."

Finally, she looked up. "Okay. So are you saying we can still be friends after all those things we said?"

I couldn't answer her.

"See? You don't think we can."

I let out a deep breath. "Yes, I do. I'm sorry. Please try to forgive me for all the things I said. I'm not dumping you." I looked at her. "And I hope you don't dump me either."

Nicole smiled. I realized it had been a long time since I'd really seen her smile. "I'm sorry too."

CHAPTER 26

Friday, July 11

I barely remember Thursday. Nic and I wandered through the day next to each other, but we weren't together.

We talked. We didn't fight or say mean things. But it didn't matter. The damage had been done. It was like we were polite strangers.

And then it was Friday, the day before camp ended. Tomorrow we'd all be going home. Late in the afternoon, a bunch of us were in the cabin, packing up trunks and duffels. Packing to go home was always a sad process, but this year it was so much worse.

I left at one point to go to Solitary. I just needed to get out of the cabin for a while. There was a time when Nic and I went everywhere together, even the bathroom.

But not anymore. As I was walking away, I heard the screen door open behind me. I looked around to see Sarah following me.

"Is everything okay?" she asked.

"No, it's not."

"Well, you're talking to each other at least. Can't you work things out?"

"It's not that easy. She's miserable and I'm miserable," I said. We could say we were sorry. We could ask to take back the horrible things we'd said. But that didn't automatically erase all the hurt feelings.

"I just want you guys to move on and get over this," said Sarah.

"I don't think we can," I told her.

"Of course you can. Just . . . keep talking to each other. Keep hanging out and doing stuff. Eventually you'll both feel better."

I went to a faucet and splashed cold water on my face. So many memories. Everywhere I went in this camp, even the bathrooms, reminded me of something.

"Big excitement over Jamie and the other counselor assistants, huh?" asked Sarah. "I wonder what the whole story is."

The counselor assistants had been caught trying to play a prank on Camp Crockett, and now they were in big trouble with Eda. They weren't the only ones in trouble. Natasha, Ashlin, and Claudia left the cabin after lights out while Jamie was away, even though Whitney tried to stop them. Now there was a new drama for Cabin 3, but I wasn't at all interested in it. I was too wrapped up in my own problems.

"Well, even though camp's almost over, Eda still wants to keep things under control. I doubt she'll really punish the counselor assistants that much," I said.

"You want me to talk to Nicole for you? Is there anything I can tell her that you're having trouble saying to her?" Sarah offered.

I thought about that for a second. "Not really. We've both said we're sorry, but sometimes that's not enough, you know?"

"Yeah, I know what you mean," said Sarah, but I could tell she wondered why she and Whitney could make up and we couldn't.

When we went back to the cabin, there was a neat pile of folded clothes lying on my bed. "I found some more of your stuff," said Nic. "Do you have anything of mine?"

"I might," I said. I rummaged through my trunk and pulled out a few of Nic's shirts and a pair of her jeans. "If I find anything else, I can always send it to you later."

"Yeah, I know. But it's easier if we sort things out now."

I nodded and turned away, acting like I was busy folding my clothes. My nose was stinging, and I knew any second I might start to cry. I didn't want my clothes back. And I didn't want to give hers back either. It seemed so final.

Why weren't things okay? We'd said we were sorry. We'd made up—I thought. Why couldn't we go back to how things used to be?

We finished packing and then left for dinner. The mood all over camp was different. People were already talking about how they'd keep in touch—e-mails, phone calls, instant messages. At dinner Eda had a bunch of announcements about girls who'd be flying out tomorrow or taking the bus.

After dinner all the campers walked down to Lakeview Rock together for the last campfire of the summer. All the campers had to wear their white Pine Haven polos and white shorts, and all the counselors were dressed in green polos. Being in the camp uniform made everything seem more serious and formal.

Lakeview Rock was a giant outcropping of rock that towered about twenty feet high and overlooked the lake. The campfire was lit in the center of the rock, and lots of girls were already sitting in a circle around it.

Sarah sat down first, and then Whitney sat beside her. I sat next to Whitney.

Then it happened. Nicole walked past the three of us so that she could sit on the other side of Sarah.

I hardly noticed when Ashlin sat down next to me. Patty had ended up on Nicole's other side. So this was how camp was going to end? Nicole wouldn't even sit beside me now?

I stared at the grass in front of me and didn't move. I wasn't breathing. I could feel Whitney and Sarah glancing at me. They both knew what had just happened.

If I got up and moved now to sit next to Nicole, what would happen? Would Nic get up and move to get away from me?

I almost did it. I would show her. We were still friends. I wasn't going to dump *her*.

But I didn't. I stayed put and didn't move. I focused on the grass in front of me. I stared at that grass until I couldn't even see it anymore.

Friends always sat together at the Circle Fire because it always got so emotional. Especially tonight, everyone wanted to be sitting next to her best friend.

I just needed to hold it in for a few more minutes. As soon as the campfire really got started, people all around me would start to cry. Then I could let it out. I stared straight ahead. If I made eye contact with any-one, I knew I'd lose it.

When the first song started, I sang along with every-one else. I knew all the words to all these songs so well, I could sing them in my sleep.

Then one speaker stood up and talked, then another. Eda always asked a few people to prepare little speeches about what Pine Haven meant to them.

Then there were a few more songs, and then Eda starting singing one of my favorite songs, "Memories Gone By." We never sang this particular song until late in the session, usually sometime during the last week of camp. We'd only sung it a few times this summer. It was to the tune of "Scarborough Fair," which was such a beautiful, mournful song, it always brought everyone to tears.

We must hold on to memories gone by
Good times, friends, forever are mine.
The times we spend at camp will not die.
Summer days suspended in time.

When we leave here we won't say good-bye
Good times, friends, forever are mine.

We'll always have Pine Haven close by.
Summer days suspended in time.

In the winter, I'll think of you then
Good times, friends, forever are mine.
Soon I know we will meet again.
Summer days suspended in time.

Now I could let it out. I didn't have to hold back anymore. Whitney patted my back while I sobbed. It wasn't embarrassing to cry so hard; almost everyone was crying now. The light from the campfire lit up everyone's faces, and I glanced over at Nic sitting beside Sarah. They were both crying too. For a second Nic's eyes met mine, and then she looked away, teary-eyed, and stared into the fire.

My heart felt like it was breaking. It was a real, physical, aching pain that I felt in my chest. It was over. Really and truly over. I knew that things with Nic and me would never be the same. Why? Sarah and Whitney could fight and get over it. Why couldn't we? Neither one of us wanted this. Did we?

It was time for the candle lighting. The counselors opened cardboard boxes and passed around white candles, each of us taking one. Eda spoke about how girls had been coming to Pine Haven since 1921. She lit her candle and then passed the flame to the counselor next to her, who passed it on to the girl beside her. One by one, the flame was passed from one candle to the next until each person in the circle was holding her lit candle in front of her.

Libby and Caroline Heyward picked up shovels and doused the flames of the campfire with dirt. Now we all sat quietly, holding our candles and looking at the little dancing flames that lit up the faces of everyone in the circle.

"Tonight on our last night at camp, I'd like you to think about what each of your flames has added to the fire at Pine Haven. And also think about what the fire at Pine Haven has added to each of your flames," said Eda.

I let the hot wax drip down my candle onto my hand. It burned a little, but not enough to really hurt. There had been happy times this summer. Lots of happy times. I'd have to remember those. I stared at my flame, wanting to burn the happy memories into my heart. My tears made the flame look blurry. I wiped my wet face with my left hand, carefully holding the candle steady in my right while I stared into the flame. I kept telling myself that looking at the dancing yellow flame would make some of the pain go away. I let out a long, shuddering sigh and the flame fluttered a little from my breath.

When camp had first started, I'd wanted everything to be exactly like it'd been in past summers. But then I would've missed out on making pot holders. Talking after lights out. Floating in the inner tubes. In lots of ways Nic and I still had a great summer together. And I didn't want to give that up.

I wouldn't have to. I would save this stub of candle in the box where I kept all my other Pine Haven mementos. The box was on a shelf in my bedroom closet at home. Inside it were lanyards I'd made at crafts, my old name tags, photos, the red notebook with THE PLAN written on the front. This year, just like every summer, I would go home and put all the things in my camp box that I wanted to keep forever.

CHAPTER 27

Saturday, July 12

For the past two years on Closing Day, I'd woken up really sad and tearful, but this morning the thought of seeing Mom and going home to all the baby preparations made me feel excited. It must have been noticeable, because Sarah took one look at me and said, "You're in a good mood."

I shrugged. "Well, I'll be seeing my mom soon—you know."

Nicole turned away while she got dressed. Her dad was picking her up today for her monthlong visit. I knew she wasn't looking forward to it, but she kept quiet. If only I could hug her and promise her that I'd text her every day. I wished I could say something to make her feel better. She probably hated me now more than ever, since I was happy to be going home and she wasn't.

After breakfast there wasn't much to do except stand around and wait for friends to leave one by one. A bunch of Camp Crockett counselors showed up to help carry luggage and trunks. I looked for Blake's counselors, but I didn't see them. I wondered if Mom and Paul would pick me up before or after they got Blake. All they'd said in their last e-mail was to look for them around eleven or twelve o'clock. That was hours away.

Whitney was the first girl in our cabin to leave. She and Sarah cried and cried as they said good-bye. "I'll see you in November," Sarah said, obviously embarrassed to be getting so emotional.

"I know, but that's a long way away," sobbed Whitney. "Who's going to make fun of me till then?"

Whitney hugged me before she got into her parents' car. "Thanks, Darcy. If it hadn't been for your intervention, we probably never would've made up. I hope you and Nicole stay in touch."

"Thanks," I told her, but I doubted that we would.

Then Ashlin left, and then Claudia. A group of us were standing around saying good-bye to Patty when I felt a hand on my shoulder. I turned around to see Nic.

"My dad's here."

I was surprised that she was even going to say good-bye to me. But I was happy, too. It would have broken my heart if she'd left without even speaking to me.

"Really? Already?" I asked. Down by the road I saw Nic's father and stepmother standing by their car, loading Nic's stuff into the trunk.

"Yeah. I have to go." Nic's face was tense. She'd cried last night at the Circle Fire, but now she was holding back the tears. I didn't want to say anything that might make her break down. I knew she just wanted to get into the car and leave.

"I hope you have an okay time at your dad's. Go ahead and use the towels, and don't worry what Elizabeth says," I said. I wanted to ask, *So, are we friends again or not?* Instead I just said, "I'll be thinking about you."

"Yeah, me too. Keep me posted on all the baby news, okay?"

"I will," I said.

She stepped forward and gave me a quick hug. I was glad she'd hugged me, because I wasn't sure whether or not I should hug her.

And that was it. She said good-bye to a few other people on her way to the car, and then she got inside and they pulled away.

I wiped tears away, but I didn't really cry too much.

Sarah was standing nearby. "You should IM each other when you get back," she suggested. "It's a lot easier talking to people that way than it is face-to-face. I'll bet by next summer, you'll be even better friends than ever."

"Maybe," I said. But I knew the truth.

Now the bus was loading, and since Natasha was leaving on it, Sarah and I went to say good-bye to her. In the group of girls standing around waiting to get on, I saw Mary Claire. She had a unicorn backpack on her shoulders, and she was carrying her pillow. When she saw me, she ran up and gave me a hug.

"Bye, Darcy!"

"Bye. I hope you had a good time at camp," I told her.

"I had a great time! Gracie and Samantha are my best friends now. I wish Nicole was riding the bus with me, but she's going to her dad's. Anyway, on the trip here, she wouldn't let me sit by her."

While Mary Claire was talking, I'd noticed something. "Cute earrings," I said, my pulse pounding a little. They were little hearts.

Mary Claire touched her earlobe. "I know. Nicole gave them to me before she left with her dad. You know what else? She said I can tell everyone that she's my stepsister now. She can be really nice sometimes."

"I know she can. If you ever have a problem, talk to

her about it. She's really good at giving advice," I said, my voice choking a little.

Eda was motioning everyone onto the bus, so Mary Claire got in line. Sarah and I stood and waved with the crowd as the bus pulled away.

And then I looked up and saw our minivan driving up the road with Paul at the wheel. "My parents are here!" I yelled to Sarah.

I raced over and opened the passenger-side door almost before the van came to a complete stop. Mom stepped out and I grabbed her, giving her a giant hug.

"You look beautiful! How do you feel?" I patted her belly, which wasn't any bigger, but I couldn't wait till it really started growing.

"Lousy. These mountain roads don't mix well with morning sickness," she said.

Blake slid the side door open and jumped out. I tried to hug him, but he ducked out of the way. He still had his stitches in, of course, but now his black eye was a yellowish green. Paul came around the van and lifted me off my feet when he hugged me. "We had to stop a couple of times so your mom could hurl," he whispered.

We all walked up the hill together to get my trunk and the rest of my stuff from the cabin. Sarah stayed down by the road, in case her parents showed up.

"We were expecting you to be crying your eyes out," said Paul. "Remember last year how we had to peel you off Nicole? I've never seen such waterworks."

"Well, Nicole got picked up early," I said, leaving it at that.

We walked into the cabin to get my stuff, but there was something lying on the top of my trunk that made me stop. It was my pot holder—the one I'd made and had given to Nicole when she gave me the one she'd made.

"What's that?" asked Mom.

"A pot holder," I said, holding it up for her to see. "We made it in crafts. I guess I forgot to pack it." I unzipped my duffel enough to stuff it inside.

Blake and Paul both grabbed an end of my trunk while Mom carried my sleeping bag and pillow. I slung my duffel over my shoulder, and we walked out together, leaving empty Cabin 3 behind.

I thought about the pot holder as we walked down the hill. A token of our friendship. Was Nicole giving it back? Or was she giving me a new token since I'd given hers to Mary Claire? I didn't know how she meant it. I could take it either way.

Maybe it was just something for me to remember her by. I decided to put it in my camp box along with the Circle Fire candle stub and this year's name tag.

Sarah's parents had just pulled up when we were loading the van, so I was glad she wouldn't be stuck here all alone.

"Thanks for everything," she said, giving me a big hug. "I'll see you next year, right?"

"I guess so," I said. "Probably." But I wasn't so sure. Maybe Mom would need my help next summer.

Libby and Jamie were the last ones I said good-bye to, and then we closed all the doors and slowly pulled away. It was sad to leave, but I felt better than I'd expected. At least I had a baby brother or sister to look forward to.

Despite everything, it had still been a good summer. And nothing could erase all the happy memories I had.

"As soon as those stitches come out, I'll start rubbing Vitamin E on the scar so it won't be so noticeable," Mom was telling Blake.

"No! I want it to look cool. I like having a scar."

"Well, it'll always be there—to remind you of your first summer at camp. At least Darcy managed to get through the summer scar free," said Mom, sighing.

I sat on the back bench so I could look out the rear window as we drove out of Pine Haven. I had so many great things to look forward to later. For now, I wanted to remember what I was leaving behind.

Sunday, June 15

This was definitely going to be the worst summer of my life.

I got out of the car and looked at all the people swarming around. It was mostly parents, but there were some other girls too, and even some brothers who looked as thrilled as I was to be here. Everyone was carrying something, and everyone seemed to know what to do and where to go. Except for us.

I just stood there holding my pillow. Then this woman who seemed to be in charge walked up. She had on a green polo shirt with a little pine tree on it. "I'm Eda Thompson, the camp director. Welcome to Pine Haven!"

My mom smiled with relief, and the two of them

started talking. Dad tried to wink at me, but I acted like I had to scratch my knee.

"This is our daughter, Kelly," my mom said.

"Hi, Kelly." The director smiled at me, then checked her clipboard. "Kelly Hedges, right? And you're twelve?"

I said yes, but it came out all croaky. I cleared my throat. "That's right."

She probably thought I didn't look twelve because I'm so vertically challenged. The director walked over to a group of people wearing green polos just like hers and motioned one of them to follow her back to us.

"This is Rachel Hoffstedder, and she's your counselor." Rachel shook hands with Mom and Dad, and then she shook my hand. She looked okay. She had really short dark brown hair, and she seemed friendly. And she was pretty vertically challenged herself. "Rachel will take you to your cabin." Then the director left to say hello to some other unhappy campers.

"Our cabin's that way." Rachel pointed up a steep hill. I could kind of see some cabins at the top of the hill, hidden in a bunch of trees. My dad was trying to wrestle my new metallic blue trunk out of the back of the car. The website had said we needed trunks to keep all our stuff in because there wasn't any place to store luggage.

"Why don't I get this end?" Rachel grabbed one of the trunk handles before my dad made a complete idiot of himself. Mom had my sleeping bag and tennis racket. I didn't have anything to carry but my pillow, which was better than nothing. At least it gave me something to hold on to.

We passed a bunch of other campers and parents going up the hill. I could tell some of them were really nervous. But then a lot of them acted like old friends. Girls kept shrieking at each other and hugging. It was beyond stupid to watch. I tried to relax my face and look casual, but my heart was pounding so hard I could feel the pulse in my throat.

What was I thinking when I agreed to this? Did they hypnotize me? Was it one of those weird parental mind control things? How had my parents ever talked me into spending a month at summer camp?

They started talking about camp back in March. They showed me the brochure and the website, and at that time it looked pretty cool. *Camp Pine Haven for Girls, located in the scenic mountains of North Carolina. A camping tradition since 1921.* Anyway, my best friend, Amanda, was going to be in Hawaii for two weeks, lying on a beach surrounded by a hundred gorgeous surfers. I figured she could miss me for two weeks after she got back from her dream vacation. In March camp seemed like a good idea. But that was March.

We walked up a dirt path and came to this big stone building with a porch. "That's Middler Lodge," said Rachel, and then we turned up another path and climbed a bunch of stone steps that went up yet another hill. There sure were lots of hills. My dad tried desperately not to pant, because Rachel wasn't breathing hard at all. She'd told us she was on the hiking staff, so she probably walked about thirty miles a day or something.

By now we were finally at the top of the hill where all the cabins were. There was a really wide dirt path, and all down one side was a long row of cabins. "This is Middler Line, and we're in Cabin 1A. You guys are in the middle between the Juniors—the little kids—and the Seniors—the oldest girls."

Rachel pushed open the screen door of the first cabin we came to, and she and my dad stumbled in and plopped my trunk on the floor. They each took a big breath.

"How many girls in each cabin again?" asked Mom.

"Eight, with two counselors. This is 1A, Kelly, and that's 1B." She waved to the left side of the cabin.

"You're number one! You're number one!" Dad

chanted. I wanted to hit him with my pillow, but I just looked around at everything.

Rachel laughed at his stupid joke, then spread out her arms. "Well, here it is. Your home away from home."

I'd seen the cabins in pictures on the website, but that didn't really give me an accurate view. I wouldn't be surprised if this cabin was built in 1921. It was all gray wood. The top half of the front and back walls were really just screens. The ceiling had wood beams across it with a couple of bare lightbulbs hanging down from them. But the weirdest thing was that there was graffiti *all* over the walls. Everywhere you looked, you could see where someone had written her name. There wasn't a blank space of wall anywhere. The website had called the cabins "rustic." "Primitive" was more like it.

"You're the first one here, so you get your choice of beds. This is mine, of course." Rachel pointed to a made-up cot against the wall. I had my choice of one set of bunk beds or two single cots next to them. They all looked uncomfortable. "The bottom bunk has extra shelf space. That's always a plus."

"Okay." I dropped my pillow on the bed.

"Let's get your bed made," said Mom. Rachel and my dad stood around looking useless, and I wandered toward the other side of the cabin, which was also full of empty bunks. And then I noticed something.

"Ah, excuse me, but . . . where's the bathroom?"

"They're not in the cabins. They're in another building down the line."

"You're kidding." I crossed my arms and glared at my dad. At home we didn't have to hike to the bathroom.

"Oh, it's not that bad." Dad tried not to smile. "It's like a college dorm. Let's see the rest of camp before your mom and I take off."

Just then another counselor and camper came in. Rachel helped them with all the stuff they were carrying. Then she introduced the counselor in 1B, Andrea Tisdale, who she said was a CA—a Counselor Assistant. I'm sure Mom and Dad were glad I didn't get her, because she was, like, in training or something. She said her activity was tennis. She was a lot taller than Rachel, and her long blond hair was in a ponytail.

As we were leaving, Andrea leaned over to Rachel and kind of whispered, "No sign of the Evil Twins yet, huh?"

Rachel laughed and shook her head. *Evil Twins?* What was that supposed to mean? My heart skipped three beats.

Rachel showed us the bathrooms. They were in

a building that looked kind of like the other cabins, except it was larger and had no screens. One side had a bunch of sinks, and the other side had a bunch of stalls. "This is 'Solitary.' And the showers are over there." She pointed to another building across from the bathrooms.

"Solitary?" I asked. I watched a granddaddy longlegs crawl down the wall of one stall.

Rachel smiled. "Yeah, that's what we call the bathrooms at Pine Haven."

"Why?" I mean, seriously. Why not just call it a bathroom?

"I'm not sure. Maybe because you're supposed to be by yourself but it's a communal toilet, so you're not really, or . . ." She just looked at me and shrugged.

Whatever. I know you're supposed to "rough it" at camp and all, but actually giving up private bathrooms, hair dryers, and air-conditioned houses with no crawly things—hey, this wasn't going to be easy. How long was I stuck here for? Four weeks—twenty-eight days. All right. Twenty-eight and counting.

After that Mom and Dad hung out for a while, looking at the camp. New campers were arriving all the time. I kept wondering about the *Evil Twins*. What was that all about? And were they in *my* cabin? The counselors had laughed about it, but that name didn't sound funny to me. I looked at all the strange faces around me. Who were the evil ones?

Then we heard a loud bell ringing—a real bell that a counselor was ringing by pulling a rope to make it clang.

"Lunchtime, Kelly. I'll see you in the dining hall," said Rachel.

Okay, so now my parents had to leave. My heart was beating about two hundred beats a minute. Dad gave me a bear hug and reminded me to write lots of long letters.

"We'll miss you so much!" said Mom. I could tell she was trying not to cry, which made me want to walk off without even saying good-bye.

"I'll be okay." My voice sounded like somebody else's. I hugged Mom really fast and then walked toward the dining hall without looking back. I could barely see it through the blur, but I blinked enough so that none of the tears rolled out.

Okay. So far, so good. I'd managed to say good-bye without crying. Much.